TEXAS DO OR DIE!

BEAR WILLIS & KIT CARSON

PETER ALAN TURNER

Published by DS Productions

ISBN: 9798399100951

1

So that's the great Kit Carson? He's a mite small for a man with such a big reputation," scoffed Eric.

"Don't be judging a man by the size of his hat, Eric. By all accounts, Carson has proven himself to be as tough, fearless, and skilled frontiersman as ever wore buckskins. I'm just surprised we haven't bumped into each other before now."

The small party of six wagons and twenty-five men, women, and children had left San Diego three hours ago. Now they were slowly winding their way east along the Old Spanish Trail, connecting California with Santa Fe, Mexican Territory, and finally to El Paso, Texas Republic. The thousand-mile trek included high mountains, arid deserts, and countless canyons.

"We've all been so darn busy getting ready for the trip

that we haven't had a chance to sit and do some serious jawing," remarked Bear.

"Well," commented Eric, "Maybe tonight."

"Yep, maybe."

They were following the same trail that the native people, Spanish Conquistadors, and fur trappers had been using for centuries. But that didn't mean the path was easier. There were still plenty of heartbreak, deaths, and broken dreams to earn the section they were traveling, the name: "The Gauntlet of Death." Still, Bear hoped it would be an easier trek than crossing the Rockies.

Suddenly, Carson riding in front, raised his hand, and the wagons ground to a halt.

"Why are we stopping?" asked Waity looking around. Up ahead, Bear could see five Mexican soldiers approaching the wagons.

"Eric, I'm going to see what's going on. I should be back shortly."

Bear nudged his mule into a gallop. Even though Bear had never seen Mexican Federales. He had no doubt that the stern-faced Captain and his four men meant business, whatever that business was.

When he reached the front of the wagon train, Kit Carson was arguing with the Mexicans. Bear didn't understand what was being said but from the tone of Kit's voice. It didn't sound good.

"What's the matter?" asked Bear.

"This officer says we owe a toll," replied Carson.

"A toll? I thought we already paid a fee to travel through this territory?"

Captain," said Kit, smiling and nodding to the officer. "He knows there's no toll. But he also knows we're Americans and have no legal standing in his country. So, either we pay the toll or turn around and return to San Diego."

"There is a third option," said Bear, "We could shoot them and dump the bodies over that cliff."

"Are you crazy?" shouted Carson.

"No, but we outnumber them, and if you can convince them I am crazy, maybe they'll let us pass."

Kit speaking Spanish, told the officer that Bear and the rest of the men wanted to kill Mexicans. The officer looked at the big mountain man. Bear stropped his skinning knife on his leather belt and grinned at the Mexicans.

The officer spoke to his men, then turned to Kit and said something in Spanish. Kit smiled and, reaching out, shook the Mexican's hand. Then, the officer barked a command, and the five Federales rode away.

"Damn, that was a gusty thing to do, but it worked," said Kit.

"You ever played poker?" asked Bear.

"I'm not a gambling man," replied Kit.

"Well, don't start. What I did was called bluffing. It's when you don't have a winning hand, but you bet like you do. The other players see you bet and drop out of the game. So, you win without having to show your cards."

Later after the wagon train had stopped for the night,

Kit and Jess Red Feather paid Bear a visit. As they approached the campsite Bear's Irish wolfhounds, Thor, and Oden, lying on either side of Bear, lifted their massive heads and growled.

"Easy now," said Bear, and the two hounds lowered their heads but kept their eyes on Kit and Jess.

"Evening Bear, Mrs. Willis. We haven't had a chance to get to know each other. Do you mind if we have a chat?'

"No, not at all," said Bear. "But first, let me introduce you to my family. My wife, Waity, and our children, Charles, Rose, and Jedediah. The tall, good-looking lad is my eldest son Eric and his wife, Sara.

Kit and Jess tipped their hats to the ladies and shook Eric's hand.

"Would you like some coffee and a piece of dried apple pie?" asked Waity.

"Thank you, ma'am. A piece of pie sounds mighty good."

"Jess and I were discussing that bluff we pulled on those Federales. They knew they had no right to force us to pay a toll. But unfortunately, most travelers will pay the toll to avoid confrontation."

"Glad I could be of service," replied Bear, "I was going to tell them that I would feed them to my dogs, but I'll keep that Ace up my sleeve for the next time."

"We might need the dogs. I wouldn't be surprised if those Mexicans showed up again," said Kit.

"I don't think I've ever seen dogs this big," commented Jess.

"They're Irish Wolfhounds. They were bred to run down and kill wolves," explained Bear.

"They can kill a wolf?" exclaimed Jess, "That I would like to see."

"Well, maybe you will," replied Bear.

"You know it's funny," said Kit, "That we never met before. Of course, I had heard stories about you, but they were so outlandish, I figured you were just another tall tale, the kind men conjure up sitting around a campfire."

Bear laughed, "Well, I heard the same about you. Folks do have a way of stretching the truth."

"That they do," admitted Kit, "But tell me, why did you leave Wyoming Territory? The law ain't after you, are they?"

"Not that I know of. We moved south because I was tired of long, cold nights freezing my behind."

Kit and Jess laughed, "I know what you mean. Well, you won't find Texas that cold. In fact, there will be times when you'll long for cooler weather and green grass."

"I hear a man can round up maverick Longhorns and claim them by putting his brand on them."

"Yeah, that's true, but it ain't as easy as it sounds. The Longhorns are mean, nasty, wild critters. The Spaniards first brought them to Texas. Some Longhorns ran away and grew wild, living in the rough country around the Rio Grande. Many a fellow has tried to start a herd by capturing the wild steers. Some succeed, and some don't. If those Longhorns don't gouge you, the Apache will. Then there's the dry, hot weather, snakes and scorpions, and all matter of little critters that can drive a man and animal insane. If that isn't bad enough, the Mexicans are always crossing the Rio Grande to loot and plunder."

"You make it sound like a losing proposition," said Bear.

"I'm just trying to tell you how it really is. I'd say for every dozen homesteaders who come to Texas seeking fame and fortune, most end up returning to their homes or finding another way to earn a living."

"My family is used to hard, honest work. But tell me about this trail we're following. What can we expect?"

"Like I told you when you signed up. It's about a thousand miles of dry, hot desert, raging rivers, mountains, and Indians. A lot of the water is alkaline and poisonous. So, when we come upon a spring bubbling out of the ground. It's best not to drink the water unless you're positive its safe."

"How about the native tribes? Are the Apache and Comanche tough as the Shoshone or Cheyenne?"

"Having fought both, I must tell you the Apache and the Comanche are ferocious fighters. We'll be traveling through their territory. Usually, one or the other is on the warpath. So, we'll have to be on our guard. Remember, Texas is a republic and not part of the United States, so we can't expect help from the US Cavalry."

"What about the Rangers?" asked Eric.

"The trouble with the Rangers is there are too few of them, and they have too much land to cover. From what I heard, the Rangers are supposed to be patrolling this trail. But we're talking about hundreds of miles of real estate. Nope, out here, a man can only depend on his gun and horse, replied Carson.

"We've been doing that for years," said Bear, "Both my wife and my daughter-in-law can hunt and shoot as well as any man. So, between us, we should have a cabin built and be rustling cattle in no time."

"Well, I wish you good luck and good night," said Kit Carson as he and Jess stood and started walking back to their camp.

"Carson seems like a good man," said Eric.

"Yep, he does," agreed Bear, "I'd like to talk some more, but these old bones of mine need to rest."

2

Three days ago, the wagon train had departed San Diego heading east to the Gila River. Then it would follow the Gila River to Yuma. Compared to what Bear and his family were used to, the first leg of the journey was an easy haul of one hundred and eighty miles. However, eighty miles from Yuma, things suddenly went south.

It was two in the afternoon of a blazing hot day. The sun had beaten down mercilessly all day long. By two, both man and beast were dog-tired. Bear and his family, used to the cooler northern Rockies, had difficulty adjusting to the temperature and bone-dry climate.

"Well, I hope you're happy," said Waity as they stopped for their noon break.

"What do you mean?"

"You're the one that wanted to go south and avoid the cold."

"I never dreamed it could get this hot," acknowledged Bear, "Maybe we're getting closer to the gates of hell."

"Seriously, Bear, this heat is taking its toll on the mules. "We'll need to find some water soon."

"Kit assured me we're near the Gila River," replied Bear.

"As hot as it is, it wouldn't surprise me if the river is boiling."

"Well, if it is, then we'll have fish chowder!" joked Bear.

Fortunately, the Gila River was not boiling. Kit decided to stop at the river for the night, "We've made pretty good time, folks. So, I think we've earned a rest. But if you plan on taking a dip in the river, watch out for water moccasins. One bite, and you're a goner."

Bear and Waity were sitting in the shade of a large oak tree. They watch the children play in the water. At their side were Bear's Irish Wolfhounds.

"Bear, I've decided I want our new home to have a brook running through the property."

"Sure, luv," said Bear, barely listening to his wife, "Whatever you say."

"And how about digging a moat around our castle and filling it with alligators?'

"Alright, if that's what you want. Wait a minute, alligators and a moat?!"

"See, I knew you weren't paying attention."

Bear was about to respond when Thor lifted his grey

head and growled. Before Bear could react, one of the boys yelled, "Snake!"

Bear looked and saw a water moccasin heading straight for the children, "Get out of the water!" shouted Bear as he rushed to the river's edge. He was about to wade into the river when Thor leaped into the water. Bear watched as the big hound swam directly to the snake. The water moccasin, sensing danger, raised its head to strike at Thor.

But Thor didn't hesitate as he bit down on the snake and began shaking the moccasin as he swam back to shore. Then, finally, he dropped the dead snake on the grass and lay beside it. Bear bent down and rubbed Thor's head, "Nice work, big fella. I would never have reached the children in time."

A crowd quickly gathered around Bear and Thor.

"That's gotta be the biggest moccasins I've ever seen." Exclaimed one of the men.

"It must be five, no six feet long, and look at those fangs!"

BEAR WAS TOO busy receiving a slap on the back from the other wagon train members that he failed to see that something was wrong with Thor.

Finally, Waity poked him. "Is Thor alright?"

Bear looked at Thor, half expecting the hound to stand up and lick Bear's face. But Thor just lay there and stared at Bear. "I think he's been bit!

"Where?" asked Waity.

"On his shoulder, see right on top of the shoulder blade."

Waity looked and gasped, "He'll be a goner if we don't do something. I saw some echinacea grow on the trail, "Charles, you and Rose go back up the trail about fifty paces. Then look to your right, and you'll see some purple flowers. Pick a bunch and hurry back!"

The children rushed off, "What can I do, Mommy?" asked four-year-old Jed.

"You have the most important job," said Waity, "Sing a song to Thor."

Jed sang while Bear wrapped a piece of cloth around Thor's jaws, "There now, big fella, this is going to hurt."

Bear drew his knife and made two quick slashes across the snake bite. Thor struggled for a second but settled back down.

"His shoulder is starting to swell," said Bear.

"Yes, that's to be expected. But I hope the poultice I'll make with the flowers will draw the poison out of the wound. I've never done this before on a dog, but it should work."

Charles and his sister ran back with the flowers. A woman supplied Waity with a small bowl and a pedestal to grind the flowers into a paste. Then Waity applied the poultice to Thor's shoulder. Finally, she applied more ground flowers to the bandage and wrapped it around Thore's body.

"There's not much more we can do except make Thor comfortable. I will change the dressing every four hours."

The rest of the wagon party went back to prepare their evening meals. "I'll stay with Thor," said Bear.

Waity started to leave when Odin, who had been watching, walked over, lay beside Thor, and began licking him.

"Well, ain't that something," said Kit Carson as he approached Bear.

"They're brothers from the same litter," said Bear, "Irish Wolfhounds may be fierce hunters, but they are also loyal."

"If you ever breed them, I want one."

"You can have the pick of the litter," answered Bear.

Bear stayed with Thor through the night. Waity had given him the poultice, and Bear had changed the dressing every four hours. A couple of times during the night, Bear thought Thor was dying. The big dog would whine and shake all over. His nose felt hot and dry to the touch. Bear bathed Thor in water from the river, and finally, the Irish Wolfhound settled down and slept.

The next morning when Kit Carson and Jess Red Feather came to check on Bear, they were surprised to see Thor lying with his head in Bear's lap.

"Well, Thor made it through the night," said Kit Carson, "I've never known anyone human or animal to survive the bite of a water moccasin."

"I think because Thor is so big that, thankfully, the venom wasn't powerful enough to kill him."

. . .

"I LIKE to leave in an hour, "said Kit.

"No problem. I'll put Thor in the wagon, and we'll be ready."

"Good, we'll start climbing into the Laguna Mountains today. These mountains are not as high as you're used to, but there are some dangerous sections."

"Hopefully, it'll be cooler," replied Bear.

"Some, but not much," replied Kit, "I have two biggest concerns: one is water. It's not so bad now, but once we descend down the other side of the Laguna Mountains, it will be even hotter, and water will be scarce."

"And the other?"

"Banditos, the hills around here are filled with banditos, outlaws. Mostly what the Spanish call Mestizos. Mixed-blood Indians and whites. They love to prey on small wagon trains like ours. So be alert and keep your firearms loaded. Except for your family, me, Jess, and a couple more men, the rest are farmers, merchants, and traders with little fighting experience. The banditos know this and will try to get us to surrender. But even if we gave up, without a fight, they would probably kill us after torturing the men and raping the women."

"That ain't going to happen, Kit," growled Bear, "My son and I have fought many an outlaw, white or red. Our wives are as good with a gun as any man. Why on the way down here, from Oregon, our ship was set upon by pirates. Sara, Eric's wife, climbed the main mast and opened fire on the pirates. Her sharpshooting saved the day. So don't worry; the Willis's won't disappoint you."*

"I never doubted that, Bear. But it was good to hear you say that. These banditos only have trade muskets. So, we have the advantage with our rifles. Also, with your permission, I like to sift the wagons around. First, Jess and I will be in front. Then I'd like you and your wife in the middle and your son bringing up the rear."

"That makes sense," agreed Bear, "My son won't like it, but he'll understand."

"MAYBE THE STORIES about the big man named Bear are true after all," commented Jess as they returned to the wagons."

Kit smiled, "I'm beginning to think that the tales we heard about Bear Willis were not only true but only told half the story."

*BEAR WILLIS: Mountain Man: Wagon Train to Hell Part Two!: A Mountain Man Adventure (A Bear Willis: Mountain Man Novel Book 11) - Kindle edition by Turner, Peter Alan. Literature & Fiction Kindle eBooks @ Amazon.com.

3

Carson was right," said Bear, "it ain't much cooler up here in these mountains."

"Are you yearning for the Northern Rockies?" teased Waity.

"No, but I would like to have carried a pocket full of ice with me just to cool me off."

"Maybe we ought to set up an ice business," said Waity.

"An ice business?" What are you talking about?"

"In the winter, we go up in the mountains and cut ice blocks from the frozen lakes. Then we haul it down and pack it into barns insulated with hay. We sell the ice to fancy folks to chill their drinks in the summer and make a fortune."

"I ain't never heard of such a thing," admitted Bear.

"That's because you were too busy worrying about Mr. Bucktooth than reading the newspapers."

"Then it's good I married you to keep me informed."

CARSON'S WAGON train had been slowly climbing the trail into the Laguna Mountains for the last two days. Any idea that the mountains would relieve them from the sweltering heat was quickly dispelled. Kit had decided they would only travel from dawn till two in the afternoon.

"If we leave early and quit before the heat builds, we'll spare our animals." He explained.

"As bad as folks wanted to reach Texas, they all agreed that Kit's order made sense. By two o'clock, man, woman, and beast were ready to call it a day.

"We'll be stopping soon," said Bear, looking up at the sun. "It's hard to believe this is the same sun that up in Wyoming in the winter would shine all day and still never warm things up."

Waity was about to reply when Jess yelled, "Hold up, we have a tree across our path."

Bear set the brake and, grabbing his Kentucky Long Rifle, walked to the front of the wagon train.

When he arrived, two men were already swinging axes trying to cut the tree in half. Suddenly gunfire erupted, and one of the axmen fell.

"Ambush!" shouted Kit, "Take cover!"

Bear ran to where Kit and Jess were hiding.

"Banditos?" asked Bear.

"It would appear so," replied Jess. They're behind some rocks up on the cliffs to our right."

"Well, I'm not going to let a rag-tag gang stop me," snarled Bear as he loaded his rifle.

"How many bad guys?" asked Eric as he reached Bear.

"Don't know for sure many six or more," replied Bear, "I'm trying to flush out the two hombres who are nestled behind those boulders to my right."

As Bear and Eric watched, the two bandits popped up and fired their muskets.

"We need to get the women and children under the wagons!" shouted Kit.

"Pa, I'm going to run back to my wagon, and when I do, those two men will try to get a shot at me."

"Okay, son, stay low and move fast!"

"One, two, three!" yelled Eric as he sprinted back to his wagon. Immediately, the two outlaws stuck their heads up. Bear took aim and pulled his trigger. He didn't wait to see the results. He knew he killed the man at this range or gave him a severe headache.

Bear quickly reloads. Suddenly a hail of lead tore through the wagon train. It was followed by cries for help as two teamsters and one woman were hit. Bear cursed as several more bullets slammed into the dirt next to him.

"Keep your head down! "Bear reminded himself. Rifle fire near him caused Bear to look to his right.

"That'll teach you to keep your head down!" shouted

Waity. His wife smiled at him as she began reloading her rifle. Bear smiled back as he hollered back. "Remember to do the same!"

Just inches from his head, a bullet hitting the wagon's bed jolted him back to the fighting.

"Kit!" yelled Bear, "We can't stay here much longer. We're like sitting ducks!"

"What do you have in mind?" asked Carson.

Trying to make his six foot-six-inch frame as small as possible, Bear scampered to Kit, "We have the advantage with these rifles. But they have more men. So, we're at a standoff as long as they have the high ground."

"What do you suggest?"

"I need three men."

"What do you intend to do?"

"We'll climb to that ridge above them and fire down on the banditos."

"Take Jess and Colm McGregor. He claims to be a good shot."

"Okay, come on, Jess. We'll grab McGregor and scamper to the last wagon. Then we'll climb up above the outlaws. Kit, have everyone with a gun firing at the banditos. That'll force them to keep their head down. Until we can get in position."

It took Bear, Jess, and Colm longer than Bear expected. But finally, they reached the top of the ridge. Cautiously they poked their heads up and looked around.

McGregor nudged Bear, "Their horses," he whispered.

Bear nodded, "It looks like they left a kid to guard them."

"I can sneak up and slit his throat," suggested Jess."

"No!" hissed Bear, "He's just a boy. I've got a better idea. Cover me."

The gunfire covered the sound of Bear's footsteps as he moved quickly up behind the boy. The Bear wrapped an arm around the lad's waist and, clamping his hand over the boy's mouth, carried him back to the others.

"Relax, son," said Bear, "We won't hurt you. I will remove my hand, but you mustn't cry out. Understood?"

The boy nodded, and Bear released his hand. "Why he can't be more than ten," said Jess.

"I'm eleven," said the boy.

"Why are you with these outlaws?" asked Bear.

The boy's bravado disappeared as he spoke. "My name is Luis Lopez. Last Spring, my mother and father died of the fever. So, my uncle, Miguel Lopez, took me in. At first, he treated me okay, but now I'm just a slave to him. He forces me to ride with his gang and watch the horses. Please, sir, take me with you."

"You stay here," ordered Bear, "We got some work to do. Then we'll talk about your future. Colm, release the horses, then join us on the ledge, and we'll pour lead down on the

Banditos.

.   .   .

COLM CUT the outlaw horses free, then joined Jess and Bear on the ledge.

"I count six men," said Jess.

"Yep, that's what I got. The rest should surrender once we shoot a couple of the outlaws. We'll fire one volley and wait to see if they surrender. Ready, aim, fire!"

Three lead balls ripped through the air, and two outlaws fell. The other outlaws looked up to see who was shooting at them.

"We have you surrounded. Drop your weapons and put your hands up!" shouted Bear.

Bear expected the outlaws to do what he had ordered. But instead, one of them yelled something in Spanish and fired his gun at Bear. The bullet grazed Bear's arm. Bear grunted and grabbed his wounded arm. Blood seeped through Bear's fingers. As he shouted back, "Okay, amigos, I warned you! Let 'em have it, boys!"

Jess and Colm fired down as Kit and his men shot up at the outlaws. This time their leader and two more banditos were wounded or dead. The remaining two immediately dropped their weapons and waved their hands in surrender.

Bear pointing down to Kit and the wagons. Making it clear that the outlaws were to climb down. Bear, Jess, Colm, and the boy, reached the wagons just as the two outlaws were tied up.

"Bear, you're shot!" exclaimed Waity.

"Just a scratch, Dear."

"That may be. Still, it needs tending to before it festers."

Bear sat on a wooden barrel as Waity cleaned and wrapped the wound.

"Thanks, Bear," said Kit, "Your plan worked." Then seeing the boy asked, "Who's the lad?"

"His name is Luis Lopez. His parents died, and his uncle took him in. He forced Luis to

ride with the banditos and care for the horses."

"Alright," said Kit, "He's free to go. But the others will swing from a rope on the first tree we find."

"You're going to hang them?" asked Bear.

"Yep, they killed Samuel Hicks and who knows how many others. What would you do? Let them go free to rob, rape and kill again?"

"No, of course not. I didn't know Samuel had died. I thought his wound wasn't fatal."

"Normally, the wound wouldn't have killed a man. But Samuel had a bad heart. So, I guess the shock at being wounded was just too much for the man."

"Then justice must be served," agreed Bear, "But Luis has no family, and he's just eleven years old. So Waity and I will take him in until we can arrange a more permanent arrangement."

That's fine," said Kit, "But if he causes any problems, we leave him to fend for himself."

" Agreed," said Bear.

4

The wagon train continued down the mountains without any more problems. Finally, they settled for the night at the foot of the mountain, near a freshwater spring. Bear watched his children and Luis play leapfrog when Kit Carson approached the campsite.

"Evening, Bear. I see Luis has adjusted to his new circumstances. I was surprised that he spoke English."

"Yeah, me too. Luis said his mother taught him English. The boy also told us how mean and cruel his uncle was and how much he hated the man."

"That's one of the things I wanted to talk to you about. I plan on hanging the surviving members of the banditos tomorrow at sunrise."

"Well, they had it coming, so do what you must do."

"I will. We must teach the outlaws a lesson, or they'll

continue to prey on innocent folks. I'm telling all the family with young'uns. They may want to leave before dawn, so their children won't see the hanging."

"Thanks, Kit, that's a good idea. I've seen enough hangings to last me a lifetime."

"Also, pass the word. Everyone is to fill every container with water. Every jug, barrel, old whiskey bottle, and anything that'll hold water. Make sure the animals drink their fill. This is the last water hole until we reach Mexicali."

"Is this the stretch of desert they call the Camino del Diablo?"

"That's right. I don't think this area has seen a drop of rain since Noah built his ark. It's hot, dry, and dusty. Nothing but sand, cactus, and lizards. This time of year, Camino del Diablo is subject to sand storms. If you see one, we'll shelter in the wagons and prey the animals survive."

"Seems like I traded one misery for another," said Bear.

'Yep, that's about the size, except sandstorms are much worse. The wind will drive the grains of sand into the tiniest opening. It'll stop up your nose, mouth, and ears in seconds. If you see one coming, soak a rag in water and wrap it around your nose and mouth. I've found men dead with their mouths and nose plugged solid with sand. The poor souls suffocated."

"Thanks for the warning. I'll pray that we don't run into a sandstorm."

"Well, I have other wagons to check on. Jess will leave with the families in the morning before the hanging. He knows the route as well as any man."

That morning, Bear and the other families with young children left before dawn. Strapped to their wagons were barrels filled to the brim with water. Luis had decided he wanted to stay and see the outlaws hang. Bear tried to get the boy to change his mind, but Luis was steadfast, "I want to see them hang, so I'll know they can never hurt me ever again."

As soon as it was light enough, Bear stood on a large rock and squinted down the trail to the east. Then he pulled out his telescope and looked through it. Finally, he sat beside Waity.

"Nothing but sand and a few cacti as far as I can see."

"Despite the heat, Waity shivered, "This ain't natural. There's no grass or trees and not a drop of water. Maybe this is the entrance to Hell."

"Well, if it is. I'll spit in the devil's eye, and you run."

Waity laughed, "Spit in the devil's eye. You know, I believe you would."

By NOON, the temperature had soared till man, woman, and beast struggled. Finally, Jess rode his mule up to Bear's wagon.

"Say, partner, I think we all need a break. This heat is wearing us down."

Jess removed his hat and wiped his forehead, "Okay, we'll wait for Kit and the others to catch up. Everyone will want to drink, but tell them to take it easy, or they'll get cramps."

Bear and his family rested in the shade of his wagon when Eric raced up on his horse, "Pa, a sandstorm is coming! Cover your mouth and nose with a wet cloth and hunker inside the wagons. Cover every opening with cloth, shirts, petticoats, dresses, and anything you can stuff into a crack or hole. Kit says this isn't a time for modesty."

"Will do," responded Bear. He helped Waity button up the wagon's canvas cover. Then Bear went from wagon to wagon to help. Finally, when he had reached the last wagon and was turning to walk back, he saw the storm. The horizon was black, with sand, grit, and dust blotting out the sun.

The sand storm bore down with a roar, loud enough to rouse the dead. Bear shuddered as he heard the roar and felt the storm's strength. Rose cried, "Be quiet, baby!" scolded her brother Charles.

"Charles, leave your sister alone. We're all scared, and it's okay to cry," said Waity, "Say a prayer that the storm will soon be over."

"Dear God, save us," prayed Bear as the storm's full force ripped through the wagon train.

Waity and their three children huddled in the middle of the wagon as Bear pulled the canvas openings as tight as possible. Then he soaked rags with water and helped Waity tie them around their children before covering their own mouths and noses.

The sound of the wind was deafening, and the grating of the sand against the canvas made Bear fear that it would tear the canvas to shreds. Wind-driven sand and dust filled the interior as the storm beat down on the settlers.

Then as suddenly as it came, the storm died. Stunned and scared men, women, and children slowly emerged from their wagons. Several people fell on their knees and prayed. Others just stood silently, trying to comprehend what had just happened. Still, others rushed to check on their livestock.

"Well, thank the Lord," said Bear, "The mules survived."

Eric patted a mule on its head. A small cloud of dust rose up from the animal's dusty coat.

Animals are smart enough to stand with their backs to the storm," said Eric as he approached Bear and Eric.

"We were lucky that it was a small storm. If'n it had lasted longer, we would have lost a lot of livestock. As it is, two mules and a horse died when the storm blocked their nose and mouth."

"If that wasn't a severe storm, I hope to God I never see a bigger one," commented Eric.

"I'll ride back and check on Kit," said Jess, "Hopefully, he's okay. Bear, please get the wagons moving, and we'll catch up with you."

Bear and Eric went back down the wagon train, urging the folks to hitch up the mules and get moving. As they neared the end of the wagons, Mabel Campbell came running up, "Have you seen Mary?"

"No, we haven't," replied Bear.

"Oh, Lord, my girl's missing."

A chill ran through Bear as he pictured the eight-year-old freckled face lost in the sand storm. But putting on a brave face, Bear asked, "When was the last time you saw Mary?"

"It was right before the storm. Mary had been playing with Jane, and I assumed she sheltered with them. But Gladys said Mary wanted to be with us. So, the last she saw of Mary, she was running back to our wagon.

"Oh my God, the storm must have swept her away!" cried Mabel Campbell.

"There now, ma'am," said Eric, "I'm sure she took refuge with one of the other wagons. Pa and I will check. Why don't you return to your wagon in case your daughter shows up? As soon as we know anything, we'll let you know."

"Thank," sniffed Mabel Campbell, "I hope you find her.

Bear and Eric checked with each of the wagons, but no one remembers seeing Mary. "I'm afraid the girl got lost in the storm and is lying somewhere dead," said Bear.

"I sure hope you're wrong, Pa."

"Well," said Bear, "Here comes Kit and crew. I'm sure they've seen her."

But as Kit rode closer, Bear got the news he'd been dreading. In front of Kit was a small bundle. The bundle was tied to Kit's saddle. Kit's hand rested tenderly on the blanket, and Bear knew Mary was dead from Carson's expression.

Kit stopped in front of Bear and Eric and dismounted. Kit slowly untied the bundle and, turning, handed it to Bear.

"We found her less than fifty feet from the train. I guess Mary got caught in the storm and became confused."

"What a terrible way to go," said Bear.

"Do you want me to take her to her family?"

"Yeah, but before we do, I'll have Waity clean her up."

MARY WAS LAID to rest in a simple grave at the side of the trail. Bear had made a grave marker with her name and a cross carved into the wood. Everyone knew that life on the frontier could be short and death was a constant companion. There was no time to grieve as the living had to get on with the task of surviving.

"I couldn't bear losing a child," said Waity as they returned to their wagon.

"Nor, I, but if it happened, we would manage somehow, just like so many others."

"It's a hard life we've chosen," commented Waity, "Sometimes I think we should have stayed in Wyoming."

"Well, there's no turning back, Waity. All we can do is

put one foot in front of the other. But, the one thing I promise you. When we get to Texas, I'll build you a home fit for a queen."

"I'd be happy living in a tepee if it meant having you and my children safe and near me."

Bear put his arm around his wife and drew her nearer, "If that's what you want. Then the first thing I'll do is put up a tepee. Now, we better hurry back, or Kit will leave us."

The days dragged by, and the relentless sun beat down on the weary travelers. As Kit Carson had warned them, the hot, dry desert weather sucked the moisture from their wooden wagon wheels, shrinking them till the steel rims fell off.

With their water supply rapidly diminishing, the pioneers took to peeing on the wheels rather than wasting precious water. Finally, with barely a drop of water in their barrels, the wagon train reached Mexicali and water.

"HOLD THE MULES BACK!" shouted Kit and Jess, "Control your mules, or they'll tear out of their harnesses and flip your wagons over!"

The mules caught the scent of the Rio Huero long before the settlers saw the river. As the wagons neared the Rio Huero, the mules started braying and straining at their harnesses. Like the people, they were desperate for water. Holding the mules to a fast trot took every ounce of strength. Even so, as Kit had warned them, two of the wagons managed to lose control of the mules, crash over the river bank, and flip sideways into the river. Fortunately, Kit, Jess, and Eric managed to right the wagons before anyone drowned.

"Let the mules drink all they want, and be sure to soak your wagon wheels till the wood swells and the rims are tight. I don't want to see anyone peeing on their wheels tonight."

Once the mules were in the water, they calmed down. This allowed the settlers to splash and bathe in Rio Huero's brownish water. Bear had stripped to the waist and was floating on his back when a squad of Federales appeared on the far side of the river.

The captain began shouting in Spanish, but the settlers paid him no mind. That is until he drew his pistol and fired three shots into the air.

"Oh, damn, "said Bear, "What did we do to upset the local law."

Bear stood and walked across the river with his wolfhounds swimming with him. At six-foot-six, the river barely reached his chest. As Bear approached the river bank, he realized he and the hounds were causing a stir.

"Well, boys, it looks like these Mexicans have never seen a real dog before. Now behave yourselves, and don't go eating any little children."

Bear climbed the riverbank as his wolfhounds raced ahead of him. The Federales and the people drew back. They had never seen anyone so big, and the wolfhounds looked like they could be guarding the gates of Hell. Most of the women made the sign of the cross and covered their eyes while the children stared in wide-eyed wonder. The men tried to look brave as they faced the Yankee Giant and his hellhounds.

Bear walked over to where Kit and Jess were arguing with the captain. As Bear approached, the Federales stepped backward and cocked their guns. The captain determined not to let the bare-chested Notre Americano intimidate him, barked an order to his troops. Reluctantly the Federales lowered their muskets and stood at attention.

Kit looked Bear up and down. At five-foot-four, Kit was smaller than most men, and standing beside Bear, the legendary scout looked like a small child.

"You sure know how to make an entrance," smiled Carson.

"It never hurts to put on a show for the locals," grinned Bear, "So what's the problem?"

"According to Captain Diago, we have violated several laws just by wading into the river. So, he's threatening us with a big fine or jail."

Bear glared at the captain, who stood only five feet tall. Bear continued staring at the captain until the man took a step back.

"Ha, won that round," thought Bear, *"Let's see if I can win round two."*

"Kit, ask the captain if he's a sporting man."

"What?"

"A sporting man. You know, the kind that likes to gamble. I have an idea that just might get us out of this predicament."

KIT TURNED BACK to the captain and spoke to him in Spanish. As the Captain listened, his eyes lit up, and a big smile creased his face, "Si. Si, deportisa!"

"He says he's a sporting man."

"Great, now tell him I'm Bear Willis, the Wild Man from the North and the rassling champion of the world. I will fight their champion. If I win, he lets us go without paying a fine or doing jail time. But, if I lose, He gets one of my wolfhounds plus twenty dollars in gold."

"You're willing to risk losing one of your dogs?"

"He probably wants my hound to fight. He doesn't know that my hounds will run away the first chance they get. So, tell him."

Kit relayed the message to the captain. This time the captain spoke to a well-dressed man standing next to the Federales. They talked back and forth, and finally, the official smiled and shook his head yes."

"The captain had to get the mayor's permission. Which the mayor readily gave him. He said the contest will be tomorrow at noon. Until then, we can drink all the water we want."

5

P a, do you know what you're getting yourself into?" asked Eric.

"Yep, a rassling contest."

"Didn't you always tell me that before making a decision, know all the facts?"

Bear put down his pipe and stared into the night sky.

"You're right, Eric, and at the time, that was and still is good advice."

"Then why did you challenge their rassling champion without knowing who he is? You ain't getting any younger; for all you know, he may be some young giant who'll tear your head off."

"You might be right, son. But if I didn't think of something, we might all be in jail and our wagons and equipment property of the city of Mexicali."

"But what if you lose?"

"In the unlikely event that I'm defeated, your mom and I have enough gold to pay the fine."

"You sound like you don't think you'll survive the match?"

"The only way I lose is if their champion kills me."

Eric realized that there was no way out for Bear. But, for all his bravado, Eric knew his father wasn't as confident as he pretended. *"Pa's putting on a brave show for Ma and the rest of the wagon train. It's true he's never lost a fight, but there's always a first time."*

Bear and the rest of the wagon train party arrived fifteen minutes early. The town's bullfighting arena had been turned into a wrestling ring. Four wooden posts had been driven into the ground at ten feet apart. Ropes had been strung around the posts, forming a square ten feet on each side. In two corners, there was a stool and a bucket of water.

The stands were already filled with people. They were some boos and jeers as Bear walked over to the ring and made a big show of inspecting the construction of the ring. Finally, he nodded and stepped inside the ring, and taking off his shirt, he paraded around the ring, flexing his muscles to the crowd's amusement.

Then as the church's bells struck twelve noon. A roar went up from the crowd as the local wrestling champion strolled into the arena. He strutted around the arena like a

game cock, waving to the crowd. Bear stood with a
bemused look. "

*He can't be more than five-eight. But his arms are so long
they almost drag on the ground!"*

Bear had been told his name was León del Mexicali or
Lion of Mexicali and that he was undefeated. Two official-
looking men entered the ring.

*"I guess one's the referee, and the other wearing the funny hat
is the announcer,"* thought Bear.

The man with the hat raised his hands, and the crowd
fell silent. Then, he motioned both Bear and the Mexican
Champion into the center of the ring. First, he spoke to the
wrestlers in Spanish, which meant nothing to Bear. Next,
he raised Leon del Mexicali's hand, and the arena shook
with the cheers of the spectators. But when Bear's name
was announced, the crowd booed and threw all sorts of
objects into the ring.

FINALLY, the announcer had had enough. He shouted
something to the onlookers, and they settled down.

Then the announcer speaking in Spanish, explained the
rules. But Bear didn't need an interpreter to tell him the
rules. Because basically, there were only two: The match
began at the sound of the bell. Secondly, the fight ended
when a wrestler couldn't get up or was thrown out of the
ring. There were no rules against kicking, gouging, biting,

or using a foreign object like a chair to beat your opponent. However, Bear knew that if he resorted to these methods, he would probably be lynched by the crowd. Of course, his opponent could and probably would use any dirty trick to win. Bear and his opponent went back to their corners to await the bell. Bear glanced at Waity, Eric, and the kids and gave them a wave and a great big grin.

Suddenly, the bell rang, and the match began. Both wrestlers started circling the ring, trying to gain an opening. The crowd grew tired of watching them chase each other and started booing. Finally, Bear went to the center of the ring and waved the Lion to join him. They stared at each other for a few seconds, then locked hands, intertwining their fingers in a test of strength.

Bear's height and strength gave him an advantage over the shorter Mexican. As Bear increased the pressure on the smaller man's fingers and hands, he looked into the Lion's eyes. At first, there was defiance, but that slowly gave way to fear as Bear's towering strength threatened to snap off the man's fingers.

Typically, Bear would force this opponent to his knees. But this time, Bear knew that if he shamed the Lion in front of his supporters, it would only bring more trouble down on him. So, Bear relaxed his grip, but that was a mistake. The Lion slipped out of Bear's hold and stomped down hard on Bear's right foot. Bear howled in surprise and pain, and the crowd cheered. Then before Bear could react, the Mexican leaped on Bear's broad back. The

Mexican reached around, hooked his fingers in the corners of Bear's mouth, and pulled.

Bear knew he only had a second to throw the Lion off his back before his mouth would be torn apart. So, Bear reached behind him and, grabbing a handful of hair, threw the Mexican from his back. The smaller man landed in a cloud of dust. But sprang quickly to his feet.

Bear, smarting from having his mouth ripped open, and his right foot stomped on, was amazed at Lion's quickness and strength. Once again, the wrestlers circled the ring. Bear, limping and bleeding from his mouth, looked like he was being stalked by León del Mexicali. However, the Mexican wrestler appeared unharmed as he skipped and did handsprings to the crowd's delight.

"Okay. Little man, I underestimated you. But that won't happen again."

Kit Carson watching the bout with Eric, said, "Your father reminds me of an old bull moose that is being hamstrung by a pack of wolves."

"Don't fret. My Pa's been in worst situations and has always come out on top," Eric snapped.

"I hope you're right. But just the same, I've told everyone to be prepared to fight our way out of town if he loses."

"I'll bet you one hundred dollars in gold coin that Pa won't lose. So, come on, Carson put your money where your mouth is."

"I'm not a betting man. I want your father to win just as

bad as anyone else. I'm just saying that time catches up with us all sooner or later."

ERIC IGNORED KIT'S COMMENT. He could tell that his father had something up his sleeve, *"Pa's pretending to be badly hurt. He's hoping the Mexican will get overconfident and make a mistake. Then Pa will finish him."*

"Come on, Pa, whup him!"

Eric had barely gotten the words out of his mouth when the Mexican circled in front of Bear and started walking backward, taunting the big mountain man. To everyone except his family, Bear seemed to shrink in size as he staggered around the ring. León del Mexicali sensing victory, moved closer to Bear.

Suddenly, Bear struck! Grabbing the Mexican like a father would pick up a child, Bear wrapped his arms around León del Mexicali in a bear hug. The Mexican, at first, tried to break free of Bear's arms. But it was hopeless as Bear squeezed. Each time the Mexican took a breath, Bear squeezed harder. Finally, the smaller wrestler stopped struggling as his head flopped to one side.

With a roar that shook the arena, Bear raised León del Mexicali over his head and tossed him out of the ring. The Mexican landed in a heap as the townspeople groaned. Then, reluctantly, the announcer entered the ring and, raising Bear's arm, shouted in Spanish that Bear Willis was the winner.

"I'm sure glad I didn't take that bet," said Kit.

"A word of advice, Carson. Never bet against a Willis because you'll lose every time."

"Eric, I sure hope this stays between you and me."

"Yeah, it'll be our little secret," quipped Eric.

Waity rushed to Bear with a jug of water and a wet cloth, "You had me worry for a moment," said Waity, "But then I saw that twinkle in your eyes, and I knew you were only playing with him."

"He's a good wrestler, strong and quick, but he has much to learn."

"Well, Pa," laughed Eric, "You gave him a good lesson."

"Yeah, but let's leave Mexicali before they change their minds."

"Un Momento, Senor."

Bear turned and stared down at the captain. The man's voice quivered as he spoke. The mayor and I have decided that your wagon train has created a public nuisance. However, because you did provide some entertainment, we will let you leave town if you give us one of your wolfhounds.

Bear's eyes flashed anger, and the captain stepped back, expecting Bear to punch him. "I know you want my hound to fight. But, if I give you my hound, you promise to let the wagon train leave?'

"Si, of course."

"Then meet me in two hours at our wagons."

The captain couldn't believe the big mountain man

would easily give him a hound. Now all he could think of was how he was the money the wolfhound would earn them.

6

The Mayor and the Captain are outside, Bear," said Waity.

"Let them sweat a while," replied Bear, "Okay, Thor, let's try this collar on. The huge Irish Wolfhound looked at Bear with trusting eyes.

"I know, big fella, but this collar just needs a few good pulls, and it'll tear open. I'll come for you tonight. Until then, try not to eat any Mexicans."

Bear exited the wagon with Thor right behind him. Standing impatiently in the hot sun were the Mayor and Captain Diago.

"Sorry to keep you waiting," lied Bear, "Thor has been a good dog, and I hate to see him go. Now, mind what I tell you. Feed him well and let him run. If you don't, he'll weaken and be no good as a fighting dog."

"I know how to raise a dog," snapped Diago, "One taste of the whip, and I'll have him eating out of my hand."

"You use the whip, and he'll turn on you. A wolfhound isn't like other dogs. There are fierce and fearless. They've been bred for hundreds of years to hunt and kill wolves. So, you've been warned. Mistreat him, and I'll not be responsible for Thor's actions."

Captain Diago grabbed the lease from Bear, "Well, he ain't your dog no more. Adios, and if you ever set foot back in Mexicali, I'll toss you in jail."

Bear said nothing. He bent down and gave Thor one last pet, "Be a good dog, Thor."

Then Bear turned and went back into his wagon. A few minutes later, Eric struck his head into the wagon.

"We're all ready to go."

"Okay, son," said Bear as he tucked a small flute into his pocket. "I'll catch up with you later."

Bear watched the wagon train disappear around the bend. Then he took his mule and walked over to a small grove of trees. He built a small fire and placed a steel pot filled with water on the rocks around the fire. Once the water was boiling, Bear removed the pot and tossed in a handful of coffee grounds. As he waited for the coffee to brew, he filled his pipe with tobacco and lit it with coal from the fire. Bear leaned back and puffed on his pipe.

"Not too bad for Mexican tobacco."

Bear drank the coffee and finished his pipe. *"Time for a siesta,"*

When he woke up, it was dark, *"I guess it's time."*

He mounted his mule and rode slowly back to town. Bear had learned that behind the jail, Captain Diago kept a kennel. So, Bear tied his mule to a fence post a block from the jailhouse and, keeping to the shadows, crept silently to the kennel.

As Bear neared the kennel, he could hear Diago curse. Bear didn't understand Spanish, but there was no misunderstanding the tone of Captain Diago's voice or Thor's growl.

Bear peeked around the corner and nearly broke out laughing. Captain Diago was pulling on Thor's leash.

"Looks like he's trying to get Thor to take a walk."

THOR WAS SITTING on his haunches. He was nearly as tall as Captain Diego and far more intimidating. Diago's whip was hanging on his belt. Then, finally, uttered another curse Diago uncoiled his whip.

"You'll never lay the lash on my dog!" hissed Bear.

He pulled the bone whistle from his pocket and blew. Diago and Bear couldn't hear the whistle, but Thor could. The Wolfhound growled, stood, and pulled hard against the leash, nearly jerking Diago off his feet. The captain dropped his whip and held onto the leash with both hands. Thor yanked his head back again, and with a snap, the collar broke. Thor charged out of the kennel, knocking Captain Diago down.

"Good dog," whispered Bear as he backtracked to his mule. He climbed into the saddle and urged the mule into a trot. By the time Bear reached the edge of town, Thor was running beside him. Bear dismounted and rubbed Thor's head, "Sorry, big fella, but I knew you could do it. Now let's find the wagon train.

The following day, Bear was awakened by Eric's voice. Bear had asked Eric to be on the lookout for Captain Diego.

"Pa, it's Diago, and he's looking for Thor. Kit and I will delay him as long as possible."

"Thanks, Eric. Waity make room for Thor."

From inside the wagon, Waity said, "Come on, Thor."

Bear smiled as Thor wagging his tail, jumped into the wagon. Bear was pouring a cup of coffee when Captain Diago and two of his men stormed into Bear's campsite.

"Where's that mongrel!" demanded Diago.

"If you're referring to Thor, he's no mongrel. He's a pure-blooded Wolfhound."

"Stop with your lies. Tell me where the dog is!"

"The last time I saw Thor, he was with you."

"He was," admitted Diago, "But last night, he escaped. He would go only one place, and that's back to you. So now, where is he?"

"Like I said, I haven't seen him since last night. But you're welcome to have a look around."

"That's what I intend to do, and if I find the hound, I'll throw you in jail!"

"Search all you want, Captain, but stay away from my wagon. Last night my daughter came down with a fever. She's been vomiting all night. My wife is in with her now."

"Fever, you say?"

"Yes, she was fine yesterday. Then all of a sudden, she and two other children are ill. My wife thinks it could be smallpox."

"The pox? Buen Dios! Alright, men, look around and report back."

"Relax, Captain, have some coffee."

"No, you might be infected,"

"No worries, I caught smallpox, so I'm immune."

"Well, I didn't," said Diago.

"Oh, that's too bad. I would hate for you to catch my daughter's illness and carry the disease back to the village."

Captain Diago took several steps back away from Bear. Then began pacing nervously until his men finally returned."

"We have looked everywhere, Captain, but we can't find the dog."

CAPTAIN DIAGO SHOOK HIS HEAD, "Willis, I know you are playing me for a fool. If I find you stole my dog, I'll have you hung."

"I warned you, Diago, not to mistreat Thor. The dog is half wild and has probably run off to the mountains."

"I think you lie, Willis. But right now, I want you and

your wagon train to hit the trail. "Thank you, Captain will be ready to leave in ten minutes."

LATER KIT RODE up to Bear, "That was some trick you played on Diago."

Bear smiled, "If I didn't call Thor probably would have torn Captain Diago to pieces."

"I must say, Bear, when I first heard the stories about you, I didn't believe them. But you've proven me wrong."

"Well, my adventures can't compare with yours, Kit."

Carson laughed, "We make quite a pair, don't we?"

"That we do!"

7

The next leg of their journey would take them from Mexicali to Yuma. This section promised to be easier than the last.

"It's only sixty miles or so," explained Kit.

"That'll be a welcome change after what we have just been through," said Bear.

"Yeah, and many folks are traveling back and forth. Once we get to Yuma, we'll need to make sure our animals and equipment are in good shape because the next section to Tucson is two hundred and fifty miles of desert, rattlesnakes, and Indians. If the desert doesn't kill you, the rattlesnakes or Kiowas will."

"From Tucson, it's another three hundred miles of some of the most desolate country known to man. The Apache roam this country at will, preying on any fool crazy enough to travel through their land."

"Sounds like it'll be an interesting journey."

"Carson laughed, "That's one way to look at it. But, of course, the only good thing is we won't have to climb any mountains."

"I guess that's something," said Bear.

"What are your plans once you get to El Paso?"

"I understand there's good land north of El Paso in the Franklin Mountains."

"I'm not familiar will the area," said Carson.

"Supposedly, it's good grazing land. My son and I plan to round up some wild maverick longhorns and use them to start a herd."

"Have you ever worked with longhorns?"

"Nope, but it can't be much different than hunting buffalo."

Carson laughed, "I don't know much about raising cattle, but from what I've been told, they're mean and hard to handle."

"Well, I guess I'll have to learn fast."

"You might want to hire some experienced men." Ranch hands who know their way around a longhorn."

"Okay, said Bear, "By the way, are you interested in working with me?

"Me? I'm no ranch hand. Besides, I signed a government contract to shepherd folks back and forth over the road we just came over."

. . .

KIT CARSON WAS RIGHT; compared to their trek's first leg, the short journey to Yuma was a walk in the park. An added bonus was meeting other travelers when they camped at night. Most were teamsters hauling goods back and forth between Yuma and Mexicali. Many had knowledge of the El Paso area.

Yuma was a smaller and tamer town than Mexicali. On Kit's advice, the wagon train stayed an extra day, ensuring each wagon was properly outfitted for the rigorous journey to Tucson. Bear decided to buy two new mules, an extra wagon axle, and two more barrels to haul water.

"I LIKE to have more barrels, but I think that would be too much for the mules."

Waity ensured they restocked their food supplies, even buying some rock candy and licorice for the children.

Two more families joined the wagon train. Kit also hired an old-timer named Pecos Jack. When Bear questioned why Kit had hired him, Kit responded, "I figure he might prove useful. Pecos is half Yaqui Indian and Mexican. Nobody, including Pecos, knows how old he is, but the man speaks several Indian languages. Plus, he tells more tall tales than you do."

"Well then, I guess we'll have plenty of entertainment around the campfire," laughed Bear.

Finally, they were ready, and at first light, the wagon train left Yuma. Their biggest fear besides the desert was the Kiowas and Apache. Both tribes were at war with both the Americans and Mexicans. Since Texas' independence from Mexico, the attacks on the settlers had increased. Because Texas was a republic and not part of the United States, they couldn't expect any help from the United States Army. Instead, the newly formed Texas Rangers had been tasked with defending the settlers and defeating the Indians. Because of the threat of attack, the settlers had stocked up on ammunition.

They were three days out of Yuma when Kit saw riders headed their way. As they got closer, Kit said, "Relax, folks, they're Texas Rangers."

The six rangers halted, "Howdy folks, where are you heading?"

"Tucson, then on to El Paso," answered Kit.

"Say," said a tall rough-looking Ranger, "You ain't Kit Carson, are you?"

"One and the same," replied Kit.

"It's a pleasure to meet you. I'm Captain William Wallace, but everybody calls me Big Foot Wallace."

"That's an interesting pistol you boys got," interrupted Bear.

"It's the latest from Samuel Colt. It's called a Patterson Colt. It's a revolving pistol and carries five bullets. A good man can fire five rounds in the blink of an eye. With Sam Colt's revolver, the Indians don't stand a chance."

"You don't say?" replied Bear, "I've got to get me one."

"Yep, if you do, get yourself the long barrel for better accuracy."

"Thanks for the advice."

"You're welcome. Now I'll give you some more advice, the Comanches are raiding all up and down the Rio Grande and North into Arizona Territory. We've been chasing a band of them around for a week. Almost caught up with them yesterday, but they slipped away in the night."

"Comanches?" said Kit, "I thought our biggest worry is the Kiowas and Apache?"

Wallace laughed. "Oh, they're still causing trouble. I'll tell ya, if the Indians ever combine forces, they would wipe us out. Fortunately, ain't none of the tribes can get along with each other."

"Well," said Kit, "If'n they did, we all be in real trouble."

"Amen to that, brother," replied Wallace, "We'll be patrolling to the north and then circling around south. So, stay alert."

"Thanks, Captain, we will," answered Kit, "And God Speed."

Captain Wallace saluted Kit, then he and his Rangers rode away.

"Be nice if they escorted us to Tucson," commented Bear.

"The only problem with the Rangers is there ain't enough of them. So, we're on our own out here."

"What are our chances of running into a band of hostiles?"

"I won't bet against it, Bear."

THE NEXT DAY, Bear and Eric were taking their turn scouting. They were about a mile from the wagons when Eric pointed to a ridge on the right.

"Pa, take a look."

Bear took out his brass telescope and peered through it, "They're Indians, alright. I can't tell which tribe they are, but they're wearing warpaint."

Best get back to the wagons and warn Carson," said Eric.

Bear and Eric wheeled their mules around and galloped back to the wagons.

Seeing Eric and Bear, Kit rode out to meet them, "You fellows riding like the devil's chasing you."

"Worse," huffed Bear, "Eric spotted a band of Indians less than a mile ahead of the wagons."

"How many?"

"Not sure, maybe ten or twelve. There were wearing war paint, and I don't think the warriors were going to a party."

"Alright, go down the line and tell everyone to keep their guns handy and close up any gaps between wagons. The Indians could be just a small band and will leave us alone. Or it might be an advance patrol of a larger force. Either way, stay alert."

"Okay, Kit," said Bear.

"Jess, let's see if they want to pàrle."

Bear and Eric watched Jess tie a white rag to his rifle. Then with a quick smile, the two men rode out to greet the Indians. Dust rose as the warriors raced down the hill and surrounded Kit and Jess, waving their rifles.

"They don't seem to be giving Kit and Jess a warm welcome," commented Eric.

"No, they don't," replied Bear, "Say, are you ready for a shooting match?"

"What do you have in mind?" asked Eric.

"I think those Indians need a lesson in marksmanship. See that shield their leader is carrying?"

"Yep,"

"Well, watch this."

Bear shouldered his rifle and sighted down the long barrel. Then, taking a deep breath, he aimed at the shield of the warrior wearing the war bonnet. Bear squeezed the trigger, and the flint struck the gunpowder. The rifle kicked back into Bear's shoulder, and the lead ball sped toward its target. The bullet slammed into the rim of the shield. Shattering it and yanking it from the warrior's hand. The startled Indian threw his hands away in surprise and fear.

"Your turn, son."

"How about the spear?" asked Eric sighting on the lance struck in the ground.

"That would be one hell of a shot," grinned Bear.

"For you, Pa, with your eyes, but not for me," kidded Eric.

Bear was going to respond to Eric's joke about his eyes when Eric fired. The bullet hit the lance halfway up its wooden shaft. Pieces of the shaft peppered the warrior's horse. The big black stallion reared up, and it was all the Indian could do to keep from falling off.

Bear slapped Eric on the back, "Damn, that was some shooting."

"Thanks, Pa. I like to see Mr. Colt's revolver do that," said Eric.

Bear laughed, "Well, let's see what the Indians do next."

The Indian leader looked back at Bear and then at his shield and broken lance. Then he shouted something to his braves, and they rode away. Kit and Jess galloped back to the wagons, each grinning from ear to ear.

"That was impressive," said Jess.

"Yep, you sure scared the dickens out of those Comanches and gave them something to think about," agreed Kit, "But I'm afraid they'll be back."

8

That night Bear found Pecos Jack sitting on a barrel and smoking a corn cob pipe. The old man gave Bear a toothless grin, "Ain't nothing better than a corn cob pipe. Too bad all I got to smoke is dried corn husks mixed with tobacco."

Bear pulled out his tobacco pouch, "Here ya go, Pecos, I'll trade tobacco for some advice."

Pecos dumped the contents of his pipe on the ground, refilled the bowl with Bear's tobacco, and lit it. He puffed a few times, "I about near forgot how good real tobacco is. Now, what is it you want to know?"

"Kit said you were familiar with the Franklin Mountains north of El Paso."

"Yep, born and raised there until we got kicked out?"

"You were forced to leave. Why?"

"Some fool found traces of gold, and before we knew it, white men came telling us the land was no longer ours."

"I'm sorry to hear that,"

"Why? It wasn't your fault."

"No, but I'm sorry, just the same."

"Thanks," replied Pecos, "Anway, we moved deeper into the mountains, and there we stay."

"Tell me about the land. Is it suitable for farming and raising cattle?"

"Well, there's no miles of open land. Most of it is either owned by the government or private individuals. Remember, the Spanish have been in Texas for hundreds of years. So, all the land has been surveyed at one time or another, and land grants have been issued giving ownership to land. This land has been held by some wealthy families for generations."

"If you want land for cattle and to build a house, you must first check with an agent to see who owns the property. Then you'll have to contact the owner and see if he wants to sell the property."

"Alright, but is the land good for raising cattle?" asked Bear,

"It depends on the land. Some areas are rocky and bone-dry. But there are places where the grass is green and plenty of water."

"Then that only leaves the longhorns," said Bear.

"You planning on rounding up free-range cattle?"

"Yep, I hear they're a lot along the Rio Grande."

"That's true, but if you want my advice, save yourself a lot of hard work and trouble and buy good beef stock. Those mavericks may be free for the taking. But that's hot, dangerous work, especially for someone you like, a tender-foot. I've seen experienced cattlemen go into the thickets where these longhorns like to live. They think money will be easy until the man or their horse gets gored. Nope, take my advice and buy a few good breeders."

"THANKS. What about the Indians? What tribes live in the mountains?"

A mix of Comanche, Apache, and Kiowa. Along with my mother's people, the Yaqui."

"I come from Wyoming and know nothing of the southern tribes. Kit said you speak several languages."

"I do. There are many smaller tribes, But the powerful ones like the Apache, Kiowa, and Comanche are the ones to watch out for. They are fierce warriors and skilled at fighting from their ponies. You would do well to avoid them."

"From what I hear, they are hard to avoid."

"This is true. The tribes are tired of being shoved from place to place by the whites, so they're fighting back. But as you know, the whites are many and the Indian few."

"The same is true up north," said Bear.

"I'm afraid the days on this earth are short for my mother's people," said Pecos.

Suddenly, a scream ripped through the ring of wagons. "Indians!"

The scream was followed by a gurgling sound, like someone's throat was being slit.

Seconds later, there were more cries followed by curses and gunshots. Then Kit Carson's voice shouted.

"Men, to your weapons! The Comanches are among us! Protect the women and children!"

Bear and Pecos jumped to their feet just as a warrior lunged at them. The warrior swung his hatchet and caught Pecos Jack at the base of his neck. Unarmed, all Bear could do was throw a hard right which hit the Apache squarely on the nose. The force of the blow drove the Indian's nose bone into his brain, killing him instantly.

Bear bent down to check on Pecos. He lifted the older man's head. Pecos coughed and, looking at Bear, said, "When I said our days are few, I didn't think it would end tonight."

Then Pecos's head lolled to one side, and he was gone. Bear laid Pecos down and yelled, "Waity, are you safe?"

"Me and the children are under the wagon."

"Stay there! Eric, son, where are you?"

"Here, Pa, by the back of our wagon. Sara and I are alright. It's hard to see, but I think I hit one of the Indians."

Bear cursed himself for not having his guns near at hand. Looking around the dying fire, he grabbed the only thing he could find that would serve as a weapon, Waity's long-handled iron spoon.

"This'll have to do," he thought as he tested the heft of the spoon. Then, from behind, Bear heard a woman cry, "No, please don't!"

Bear spun around and saw a Comanche trying to drag a woman towards a gap between the wagons. Bear rushed at the brave, swinging his spoon. But before he could reach the Indian, Thor leaped out of the shadows. The Irish Wolfhound clamped his jaws on the warrior's arm and bit down. The Comanche grunted and let go of the woman. With his free hand, he grabbed his knife and raised it to slash at Thor. But before he could, Bear hit the Comanche on the head with the iron spoon. The Indian collapsed in a heap. Thor saddled the warrior and growled, "Good Boy, Thor."

Bear helped the woman to her feet, then pushed her under the wagon with Waity, "Stay put!"

Two more Comanche rushed at him with knives flashing. Bear hit one of the braves on his wrist, crunching bones and getting a cry of pain from the warrior. The second warrior, cautious after seeing Bear in action, circled him, staying out of range of the iron spoon.

"I love to dance with you, but I just don't have the time," snarled Bear as he jabbed the Indian in the gut with the spoon. Then as the warrior bent over, Bear whacked him on the back of the neck, and the Comanche fell to the ground and didn't move.

It was over as quickly as it had begun. Men appeared with torches and searched the wagons for any more Indians. Having seen his wife beaten to death, one enraged man was shooting every wounded Comanche.

Bear grabbed the man's arm and wrenched the pistol away, "That's enough, killing Jacob. We'll drag the dead and wounded Comanches into the brush; their people will come for them."

Bear checked on Waity and the children. All were safe. As were Eric and his family. Unfortunately, not everyone fared as well. The Indians killed three men, a woman, and a young boy.

"What did we ever do to them?" wailed the dead boy's mother. "If they came asking for food, I would have given it to them. But, instead, they come out of the dark and slaughter my boy, and for what? He ain't never done nothing to them?"

Finally, her husband approached the grieving mother and, wrapping his arms around her, helped her back to their wagon.

The dead were quickly buried in unmarked graves. So as Kit explained, "The Comanche wouldn't be able to dig the bodies up and mutilate them."

Eyes were wiped dry, and the wagon train moved on toward Tucson. After the attack, every man kept a gun nearby. Watches were posted every night, and scouts were sent out ahead of the train. They ran into Captain William Wallace and his Texas Rangers a day later.

"A fine time for him to show up!" scoffed Waity.

"The man can't be everywhere," replied Bear.

Waity wasn't the only one upset with the Rangers. Just as Wallace dismounted, he was verbally attacked by the women who lost their husbands. First, Kit and Jess had to physically restrain the grieving widows. Then just as Kit and Jess were escorting the wives away, the mother who lost her boy ran up to Wallace and began beating him on his chest.

Wallace stood there as the woman pounded on his chest. Finally, Waity pulled her away. Overwhelmed with emotion, the mother collapsed on the ground. Her husband rushed over and helped his wife up.

"Damn you, Rangers! You're never around when we need you!"

Bear could tell that Wallace was taken aback by the attacks. Wallace pulled a handkerchief from his pocket and blew his nose. Then, finally, he collected himself.

"Folks, I'm terribly sorry we couldn't rescue you from the Comanche. But the truth is we can't be everywhere. Two days ago, a band of Apache attacked the town of Rattlesnake Junction and killed ten people. Then they burned the town to the ground. We've been tracking the Indians when we heard about your misfortune. However, I pledge we'll catch up to the Indians who attacked you."

Most folks seemed to understand, but some were still livid, "That's the problem!" shouted a man in the back, "Everyone is sorry, but nothing is being done!"

"Friends," said Wallace, his voice hard, "As I said the other day, we can't be everywhere. Currently, we're undermanned. We need everything from men to ammunition to decent horses."

"So, if you want more protection, send a letter to President Steven Austin and the state legislature. Tell them to hire more men to eliminate the Indian problem, once and for all. We know who attacked you, and I promise we'll bring them to justice. But these are dangerous times. So be ready and prepared for attacks day or night."

Wallace shook Kit's hand, mounted his horse, and rode off with his men.

"Alright, folks, you heard Wallace. I think our biggest threat is at night. The Indians have seen how effective our rifles are at long distances. As I've said before, keep your guns close and your loved ones closer."

Carson approached Bear, "Bear, Jess, and I have been thinking. We need to send out long-range patrols, and as Jess and I are the only ones who know this country, we'll do the scouting. We'll try to stay around two or three miles of the wagons so we can ride back quickly if there's trouble. While we're gone, we like you and your son to ramrod the wagons."

"Sure, Kit; anything we can do to help."

"Thanks. Also, keep up the regular patrols. But make sure they stay within eyesight of the wagons.

"Will do,"

An hour later, Kit and Jess headed out. "I get the feeling that Carson's expecting trouble," said Waity.

"Yep, I agree. Kit's been nervous about something ever since Captain Wallace showed up."

"Did he say anything to you?"

"Nope, and that's what's got me worried. It ain't like Kit to keep secrets," commented Bear.

"Well, whatever it is, Kit must have his reasons," replied Waity.

"I guess," said Bear, "It's just that I figured he knew me well enough to let me in on whatever information he had."

9

The following day, the wagon train awoke to the sound of distant drums. Kit and Jess rode out to investigate. Then an hour later, Kit and Jess came over the hill at a gallop.

"Apache!" yelled Carson as he skidded to a stop. "Get these wagons moving! If the Apache catch us out in the open, we're dead. There is a dry river bank up ahead where we can defend ourselves. Jess and I will try to slow the Apache. Now get a move on!"

Men cursed and cracked their whips. Soon, the wagons were racing across the prairie. They were halfway to the river when a man hollered, "Indians coming over the ridge!

Bear's blood ran cold as he saw the Apache. Good God, there must be ten braves!"

"Waity, take the reins! I'm going to the back of the wagon with our rifles."

As Bear crawled through the wagon, he gathered the children into the middle of the wagon's bed and piled boxes, a chest, and blankets around them. Then, he quickly kissed each girl, "Charlie, come with me."

"Where are we going, Pa?"

"To save your mother and sisters."

Bear handed Charlie a pistol, "Only use this as a last resort."

Bear had always been honest with his children, "Growing up on the frontier, you children need to know how to take care of yourselves."

Bear taught his children how to shoot and survive in the wild from an early age.

"Charlie, you remember what I told you about shooting?"

"Yes, Pa," said Charlie, "His voice quaking."

"Good, now a man on horseback ain't no different than a running deer. At least as far as leading your target."

"Yes, Pa, I know."

"Good, now all I want you to do is load the rifles. But just in case you have to, remember to lead the target."

"I will, Pa. You can count on me."

"Good lad, now keep your head down."

Bear yelled at James Murdock, who was driving the wagon behind him.

"James! Pass the word! Tell the men to get in the back of their wagon so they can shoot the Apache!"

Murdock waved and handed the reins to his wife.

Then above the din of creaking wagon wheels, men's curses, and children crying, Bear heard the Apache.

"This must be what Hell sounds like," hissed Bear as he lifted one of the rifles.

Suddenly, the Apache were upon them. Bear fired, and the lead warrior fell to his left.

Charlie handed Bear the second rifle and started loading the first. Bear waited for another Apache to show himself. Then, to his horror, he saw a warrior emerge from the wagon behind him. The wife was sitting in front and hadn't noticed the Apache behind her.

BUT SHE DUCKED when she saw Bear lifting his rifle and pointing it straight at her. Bear pulled the trigger and shot the Apache in the chest. Knocking him back into the wagon.

"The bastard must have killed James," thought Bear as Charlie handed him a reloaded rifle.

"Good job, son."

The words were barely out of his mouth when an Apache rode between the two wagons and leaped into the wagon, knocking Bear backward. The Apache raised his knife, ready to plunge it into Bear's heart. But instead, Charlie fired his pistol, hitting the warrior between the eyes. For an instant, the Apache looked surprised. Then, Bear kicked the Apache in the chest, and he tumbled out of the wagon.

"Charlie, are you alright?" asked Bear, turning to look at his son.

Charlie stared blankly at the still-smoking pistol.

"Charlie!" snapped Bear, "Stay with me, son!"

Charlie's eyes focused on Bear, "Huh,"

"It's all right, son. Just concentrate on loading the rifles."

Charlie nodded, "I'm okay, Pa," said Charlie as he took the rifle.

"Willis!" yelled Kit, "The riverbank is just ahead of you. Stay on the trail, and you shouldn't have any trouble. Form a firing line and get all the women and children to shelter under the wagons."

"Where are the Apache?"

"That was just the scouting party. The main body is about ten minutes behind and coming fast.

Bear saluted Kit. Then shouted to Waity, "Hon, slow the wagon. The river bank is coming up!"

Fortunately, the trail had worn down the riverbank, so all the wagons could descend onto the dry riverbed without mishaps. As soon as the wagons were safe, Bear ordered the men to form a firing line behind the riverbank.

"Eric, do a quick head count and report back to me. Then calling to his wife, Bear said, "Waity, gather all the women and children and get them under the wagons. Hurry now; we don't have a minute to spare."

Eric returned with his report. "We were lucky, only one dead and two wounded."

"Thank the Lord for small favors."

"Then Bear looked around, "My dogs, Thor and Odin. Have you seen them?"

"Yep, smiled Eric, "There were with me when the Apache attacked. They ran alongside the Apache and harassed their ponies. Thor even dragged one warrior from his horse."

"Is that right?"

Just then, Thor and Odin came around the corner and tails wagging. Bear could see blood stains on both of his dogs."

"There you two are," said Bear as he was smothered by the two hounds, "Okay, fellas, I'm happy to see you, but we have to be ready for the next attack."

Kit and Jess were already positioning the wagons when Eric and Bear approached,

"Bear," said Kit, "Make sure all the women and children are under the wagons."

"All but my wife, Sara," interrupted Eric, "She's a crack shot, and right now, we need everyone who can shoot on the line."

"Okay," agreed Kit, "Perhaps we should check and see if any other women can handle a gun."

"Waity's a fair shot, and I believe Maureen Addison and Mrs. Carmicheal can also shoot," added Bear.

"Then, by all means, hurry up. The main body of Apache will be here any minute."

Five minutes later, Waity, Sara, and four other women were taking their position when a war whoop pierced the air.

"Here they come!" shouted Kit as he fired his pistol at an Apache Warrior. The wounded warrior stumbled backward only to be replaced by two more Apache braves. Two warriors raced their horses directly at the settlers. At the last moment, they jumped over the barricades and landed among the women and children hiding under the wagons. One of the warriors backhanded an older woman and grabbed the young girl she was protecting.

Eric ran to help the girl when he was struck by a war club. Eric stumbled. He tried to raise his arm to shoot the warrior, but his arm numbed from the war club's blow, causing him to drop the pistol. Sara seeing what was happening, fired her rifle from the hip. The bullet tore into the Apache's side, causing him to release the girl. Sara rushed to Eric's side and helped him back to the riverbank.

"Are you alright?"

"I will be. The club knocked me on my shoulder, and I lost feeling in my arm. But it's starting to come back."

The couple didn't get a chance to rest as more Apache attacked the settlers.

"Make every shot count!" shouted Kit Carson.

The intense, accurate gunfire finally forced the Apache

to withdraw, allowing the wagon train time to reload and tend to the wounded.

"It ain't over, folks!" yelled Kit, "We put up a good fight, but there are more Indians on the ridge."

Down the riverbank, the men and women rested. Bear was reloading his rifle as Kit approached, "I'm not sure we can turn back another attack," said Bear.

"I'm not sure either," agreed Kit, "Jess and I figured there were at least sixty Apache."

"Our chances don't look good, but we'll fight to the last," replied Bear.

Kit sadly shook his head, "Sorry it had to end this way."

"It ain't over yet!" growled Bear.

"I hope you're right. But just the same, make sure you save a bullet for yourself, Bear. You don't want to be captured by an Apache."

Bear and Kit shook hands, then Kit walked away.

Waity gently touched Bear's arm, "Kit looked worn out."

"Hmm," replied Bear, "He doesn't think we're going to survive the next attack."

Waity hugged Bear, "Then he doesn't know," replied Waity.

"Know what?"

"That Bear he no die."

Bear gave Waity another hug, "Go, protect the children."

10

W aity's words reminded Bear of his first wife, *Little Sparrow. It was she who first said, "Bear, he no die."

"That was a lifetime ago," Bear thought, *"Maybe we should have never left Wyoming. Maybe Little Sparrow's spirit is still up North and can no longer protect me."*

Eric interrupted Bear's thoughts, shouting, "Here they come again!"

Bear looked as down the ridge poured the Apache. *"Good God, they're more than we thought!"*

Bear shouted to Eric, "Son, aim for the leaders."

"Okay, Pa, I'll take the ones on the left."

"Steady now they're almost in range."

Even though the Apache were still out of range of most of the guns. Bear, Eric, and Sara could hit a target at three hundred yards with their Kentucky Long Rifles. Before Bear could shoot, he heard a rifle boom and watched an Apache Chief fall from his horse.

"Damn good shooting, Eric!"

"That wasn't me. It was Sara,"

"You married well, son."

"Yep, I sure did."

"You two shut up and start shooting!" shouted Sara.

Bear and Eric both fired at the same time, and two more chiefs bit the dust. When Sara picked off a fourth Apache, the rest of the warriors heeled their horses around and rode back to the ridge.

All down the line of defenders, a cheer went up. As the cheer died, Bear heard Kit shout. We turned them back, but we haven't defeated the Apache."

"That was some shooting, Bear," said Kit.

"Don't thank me. It was Sara's shooting that turned them back."

"When it comes to straight shooting, your women are equal to any man."

"Yep, and then some."

"With Sara's shooting, we may win this battle yet," said Kit.

"Never underestimate a Willis, man or woman."

"I sure won't," promised Kit.

. . .

It took the Apache an hour to regroup and launch another attack. But instead of rushing directly at the wagon train. The Apache split into two groups and charged from the right and left flank.

"I'm low on ammunition," shouted Eric.

Bear tossed his son an extra bag of powder, "That's the last of it!"

Up and down the line Bear could hear men yelling for more ammunition. Unfortunately, there was none.

*Amazon.com: Bear Willis: Mountain Man: The Making Of A Mountain Man (A Bear Willis: Mountain Man Novel Book 1) eBook : Turner, Peter Alan: Kindle Store

"It's going to come down to hand to hand," thought Bear grimly as he touched his knife and hatchet tucked into his belt.

"Let the bastards get closer and fire on my command!" ordered Kit.

"He wants to make every shot count," hissed Bear as he sighted on an Apache.

Then with the Indians almost on top of them, Bear heard the sound of pistols and men shouting. Captain Big Foot Wallace and his Rangers were sweeping in from the north. They were firing their Colt pistols with deadly effect. The men and women behind the riverbank cheered as they also began shooting. The Apache, caught in a cross-fire, finally gave up the attack and scattered. The Rangers gave chase as the Indians rode back over the ridge.

"We did it!" shouted a man. "We beat the devils!"

"Thank God for the Rangers!" yelled a woman.

The wagon train members cheered as they realized the fight was over. Now came the grim work of burying the dead and caring for the wounded.

Bear and Eric were helping an injured man to the makeshift shelter that Waity, Sara, and the women had set up. They laid the man on a blanket when Eric said, "Here comes the Rangers."

A cheer went up from the weary defenders as Captain Wallace and his men rode into the camp. The Rangers dismounted and were immediately surrounded by men and women. Everyone wanted to thank the Rangers and shake their hands. Big Foot Wallace raised his hands.

"Thanks, folks, but we were just doing our job."

"Your pistols saved the day," said Kit.

"Glad to be of service. We've been hunting this band of Apache for days. But after the licking you gave them, I don't think we need to worry about them for a while," said Captain Wallace.

"Well, we appreciate your help," said Kit.

"By the way, if I remember right, you folks are headed for Tucson."

"Yep, and then on to El Paso."

"I don't suppose you wouldn't mind if we tagged along, as least as far as Tucson?"

"Nope, we'd be glad to have the company," said Kit.

So, Captain, the Mexicans don't mind the Rangers crossing into their territory?" asked Bear.

"Officially, they do, but Texas and Mexico are at war with the local tribes. So as long as I'm chasing the Indians, I can come and go as I please."

THEY SPENT the rest of the day tending to the wounded, burying the dead, and making necessary repairs on the wagons. Later Bear and Eric stopped by the Ranger's camp.

"Evening, men," said Bear, "I was wondering if I might get some advice."

"I don't suppose it has anything to do with shooting, does it?" asked Captain Wallace.

Bear laughed, "Nope, but I'd gladly give you all some tips."

The Rangers laughed. Then Captain Wallace said, "So if it ain't about shooting, what can we help you with?"

"Well, me and my son plan to start a cattle ranch in the Franklin Mountains, and we were wondering if any of you men know the area?"

"Carl, ain't you got a brother down there?" asked Captain Wallace.

"Yep, I do. Ben has a small tin mine up on the Coronado. I doubt the area is any good for raising cattle. Too hilly. You be better off looking for land to the east."

"You and your son have any experience raising cattle?" asked Captain Wallace.

"Nope, we're just looking for a way to earn a living."

The Rangers laughed, "It's a hardscrabble land," commented Wallace, "All the good land has been gobbled up. Your best bet is working for a rancher and learning the business."

Again, the Rangers laughed, "I don't see Bear Willis as a farm hand," said Carl.

"You know, Bear with your skills as a mountain man. You and your family could carve out a living up there in the mountains. There's gold, not much, but enough to provide your family with the necessities."

"The Rangers could always use a good tracker," said another man.

"Ha," laughed another, "Willis doesn't know the land."

"I ain't never been lost," bragged Bear, "Besides, as far as I know, a man's footprint looks about the same wherever you go."

"Wait a minute," said Carl, walking over to his saddle-bag. The Ranger pulled out a small notepad and the stub of a pencil. Carl sat down and drew a map on the pad. Then he tore off the page and handed it to Bear.

"My writing ain't the greatest, but that's my brother's name and directions to his mine. If'n you get lost. Just ask around. Everyone knows him."

"Thanks, Carl. I appreciate it."

BEAR AND ERIC returned to their wagons, "Well, Pa, sounds like the cattle business ain't for us."

"Maybe not. But we'll look up Carl's brother, and who knows, perhaps we'll strike it rich prospecting for gold."

11

Thankfully, the rest of the journey to Tucson was uneventful. Captain Wallace and the wagon train camped a short distance from town along the Santa Cruz River. Here the weary travelers finally had a source of plentiful, clean water. Bear and Kit thought they had finally found a place where folks could rest and recover in peace. Unfortunately, several women had other ideas.

"Mr. Carson!"

Kit and Bear stopped as three women and a Mexican man marched over.

"Looks like trouble," said Bear.

"Now, Bear, let's not jump to any conclusions."

Kit tipped his hat, "Evening. How can we be of service?"

"Well," said Maude, "First, you can deal with Mr. Lopez.

He claims he owns the land we're camped on, and either we pay him for using the land and water or leave."

Kit put on his best smile and shook Mr. Lopez's hand, "I'm sure we can work something out? Was there anything else?"

"Yes, the ladies wish to bathe. However, some boys have no respect for a woman's privacy."

Bear raised his hand, "Say no more, ladies. "My wolfhounds and I would be glad to guard you while you bathe."

"Thank you, Mr. Willis, that's most kind."

"Is there anything else?" asked Kit.

"There is. It is our understanding that there are quite a few establishments that offer drinking, gambling, and female entertainment. So, we would like you to prohibit the men from visiting these places."

Bear tried not to laugh as Kit cleared his throat, "Ladies, I agree that these establishments should be avoided. But I can no more stop a man from going to them than I can stop the sun from shining. The best thing to do is for each of you lovely ladies to address the issue privately with your husbands."

"Well, then, perhaps we will!' huffed Maude.

Bear and Kit watched as the ladies departed. Bear grinned, "I'm thinking we haven't heard the last of this."

"Yep, I'm afraid we haven't."

"Now, Mr. Lopez, let's see if we can agree on using your land and water."

. . .

THAT EVENING, Bear and Waity and their hounds stood guard while the women bathed.

"Are we going to stand guard for the men?" joked Waity.

"Nope, you ladies can peek all you want," laughed Bear.

Waity poked her husband in the ribs, "You're an evil man Mr. Willis."

Bear put his arm around his wife, "I am," he chuckled, "But let's keep it a secret."

"DID Kit and Mr. Lopez reach an agreement?"

"Yep, Lopez is a reasonable man, and his fee was fair."

"Now all Kit has to do is keep you, men, out of those dens of sin."

"Well, as Kit said, that's up to each wife to address that with her husband."

"Ha, not until you take a bath," commented Waity.

"Okay, I'll hold you to that. I plan to wash up as soon as the ladies are finished."

LATER WAITY SNUGGLED CLOSE to Bear and asked, "Did you have your talk with the Rangers?"

"Yep, and according to them, the Franklin Mountains is no place to raise cattle. In fact, they made it very clear that without experience, I should stay away from cattle ranching."

"Hmm, then what should we do?"

One of the Rangers has a brother who owns a tin mine. He suggested I look him up. Maybe Eric and I will become miners."

"Ha, I don't see you grubbing in some dark hole in the ground. There must be something else you could do?"

"Yeah, another Ranger suggested panning for gold. Then a third said, I could hire out as a tracker and guide."

"But you don't know the land?" objected Waity.

"That's true, but it wouldn't take me long to get a lay of the land. While I'm exploring, I could earn some money as a market hunter."

"So, I guess the idea of living the life of a rich cattle-man's wife is out of the picture."

"At least for now," mumbled Bear as he stifled a yawn.

THREE DAYS LATER, the wagon train pulled out of Tucson, headed for El Paso. Captain Wallace and his Rangers agreed to accompany them, "I got orders to proceed to the border, so we might just as well tag along," said Wallace.

"Glad to have you with us," replied Kit.

With the Rangers adding their firepower, the settlers felt that the rest of the journey would be problem free. Unfortunately, that wasn't the case. Three days out of

Tucson, Bear woke up to the sound of thunder, "Looks like we're in for some rain."

"That would be a welcome relief. We haven't seen a drop in days."

"Yep, and hopefully, it'll cool things down."

Dark clouds billowed all around them, and flashes of lightning streaked across the sky, but no rain.

"The storm might blow right by us," commented Kit as he rode down the line of wagons.

"Yep, you could be right," said Bear.

But then the wind shifted and brought the rain. At first, it came down in big drops that formed little pockets of water everywhere they landed.

"Is that all?" asked Eric, "All the huffing and puffing, and all we get is a few drops?"

The words were barely out of his mouth when the skies opened up, and a torrent of rain engulfed the wagon train. Within minutes the dusty trail had turned into a river.

SUDDENLY THE TEMPERATURE DROPPED, and hail the size of apples began pelting men, women, and animals. Then the wind shifted again, and the hail turned to torrents of rain.

"This must be how Noah felt," thought Bear.

The downpour continued for several hours, turning the trail into a quagmire. Wagon wheels sunk up to their hubs and stopped, trapped in a sea of mud. Men cursed, and whips cracked, but it was no use. The mud was like thick glue. It struck to the wheels and held them fast.

Bear climbed down from his wagon and immediately sunk past the tops of his boots in mud and water. "Waity lay on the whip while I push," yelled Bear.

He sloshed to the rear of the wagon and pressed his shoulder against the back.

"Now, Waity," he yelled. Bear pushed with all his might while Waity cracked the whip and cursed like an old teamster, but it was useless. They, like all the wagons, were stuck.

"Ain't no use!" yelled Bear, "We ain't going anywhere until the road dries out."

The problem was the rain didn't stop. It continued through the day and into the night.

Bear had resigned himself to waiting out the rain. He, Waity, and their three children stayed in the wagon. They played cards and told stories well into the night. Bear fell into a fitful sleep. Sometime in the early morning hours, Bear awoke.,

"Am I dreaming, or is the wagon rocking?"

Then he heard a shout that sent chills through his body. "Help! We're being swamped!"

"Waity, wake up! We have to get out of the wagon!"

Bear jumped out of the wagon and into waste deep water. Waity handed Rose to Bear, and he carried her to the waiting arms of a Texas Ranger.

"We're taking the children to higher ground," shouted the Ranger, pointing to a nearby hillside.

Bear nodded and went back to the wagon. Waity and Bear carried Jed and Charlie up the hill. The Rangers had erected a shelter using a spare wagon cover.

"We need to unhitch the mules, or they'll drown!" shouted Kit.

The men returned to the wagons and released the mules from their harnesses.

"I thought the Lord promised Noah that he wouldn't flood the earth again," said a woman.

"Don't worry, Martha. It can't rain much longer, said her husband."

No sooner had the husband spoken than a cry went up.

"The wagons are floating away!"

The people watched helplessly as the wagons began to float away. Then when things couldn't get any worse, one of the wagons tipped over, causing the other wagons to do the same. Personal items, trunks, blankets, bags of flour and beans, and even slabs of bacon spilled out of the wagons.

"Oh Lordy, Lordy," cried a woman, "Why are we being punished?"

She started to run down the hill but was restrained by Kit.

"There's nothing we can do until the rain stops!" yelled Carson.

There was nothing anyone could do. So, the people huddled on the hill until the rain finally stopped.

By MID-MORNING, the gully washer had been reduced to a light shower, and the sun was peeking out by noon. However, it wasn't until two days later that the flooded road was finally dry enough for the wagons. While waiting for the mud to dry, the settlers salvaged what they could of their supplies. The mules had been rounded up. Fortunately, all had survived, and the wagons, although soaked and muddy, were in good shape.

"It could have been worse," said Eric.

"How in the dickens could it have been worse? I lost my rifle, all my tobacco, and a jug of Uncle Bart's whiskey!" complained Homer Evans.

"You should be thanking the good Lord that you weren't drowned!" snapped Helen McCormick.

"If'n I lost my whiskey, I might as well have."

Helen walked away, shaking her head, "She's an easy one to rattle," grinned Homer.

Eric just laughed and returned to scrapping the mud out of his wagon. The next day, Kit Carson called a meeting.

"Folks, we'll spend another day preparing for the rest of our journey. We were fortunate not to have lost anyone. The only real problem is our food supply. What wasn't washed away is unfit to eat. Captain Wallace has kindly volunteered his men to go on a hunt, so at least we should have meat. He's also sending two men to El Paso, where they will buy flour, beans, coffee, and bacon. It's about two hundred miles to El Paso. That's a four-hundred round trip. Even if they ride flat out, it'll take them eight to ten days to make the trip. So, will all have to tighten our belts until they return. I estimate that we should reach El Paso in twenty days or so. The captain tells me that the rest of our journey should be uneventful. Let's pray that he is right."

12

By the time they finally reached El Paso, Bear, and his fellow travelers looked like they had been through a war. In a sense, they had, from battling Apache to fighting the elements. The folks had dealt with the worst nature and hostile Indians could throw at them. When they left California, the pioneers were hopeful and excited about their journey to El Paso. They were exhausted but proud that they had survived the arduous trip.

"Well, Bear, I guess this is so long for now," said Captain Wallace, "But I got a feeling we'll see each other again."

"It's been a pleasure riding with you and your Rangers. Once I get settled, give me a holler if you need a tracker."

"I'll keep that in mind."

Bear shook Captain Wallace's hand.

"Hey, Pa, I've been thinking, maybe I'll join the Rangers."

Before Bear could reply, Sara said, "Over my dead body! You got responsibilities, and if you think I'm going to stay home while you go galivanting all over Texas, you got another thing coming!'

"Well, laughed Bear, "I guess that's the end of that."

"I was just joking, "said Eric.

"Well, I hope so. Now come on, you promised the children, you would buy them some penny candy."

"I guess we know who wears the pants in that family," commented Waity as she tucked her arm under Bear's arm.

"Yep, you taught her well," grinned Bear.

"Here comes Kit Carson. Remember what you promise me, and don't volunteer for more work."

Bear squeezed Waity's hand, "Howdy Kit, you look mighty pleased with yourself."

"I'm just pleased to finally be in El Paso. I've made many treks, but this one has to be the most difficult. I can't thank you and your family enough for helping out. I don't think we would have made it if it weren't for you."

"You and Jess deserve most of the credit. We just tried to be helpful."

"No, you were more than helpful. Good luck to you and your family, and if you ever need anything, I travel back and forth to El Paso every few months."

"Thank you, Kit."

The two men shook hands. Then Kit mounted his horse and rode off.

"You made two powerful friends, "said Waity.

"A man can't have too many friends. Now let's go buy us some candy."

Two days later, Bear and Eric were following the map that Carl had given him. Their wives and children decided to stay in El Paso and await their return.

"According to Carl, the mine is over the next ridge, "said Bear looking at the map Carl had drawn.

Eric shook his head, "I sure hope you're right because I can't make any sense out of those hen scratchings."

Bear was about to reply when a bullet ricocheted off a nearby rock. Both Eric and Bear ducked as another bullet narrowly missed Eric's head.

"If that's Carl's brother, he sure knows how to make you feel welcome," said Eric.

"He's just protecting his property," said Bear, "I'll call out to him and let him know who we are."

Bear cupped his hands around his mouth and shouted, "Keith! My name is Bear Willis. Your brother Carl said to look you up."

Instead of words, bullets were the answer, "Is the man deaf?" asked Eric.

"No, he's probably not used to folks showing up at his mine. Let me try again."

This time Bear stood and shouted, "We were with Carl and his Ranger unit from San Diego to El Paso."

Bear and Eric waited. "For what seemed like an eternity. Finally, a man yelled, "Drop your weapons and walk slowly toward the two mountains," ordered a voice.

Eric and Bear did as they were told. They had walked for about five minutes when suddenly they were surrounded by three heavily armed men.

"This doesn't feel right," warned Eric.

"Maybe not, but what choice do we have?"

Bear put on his best smile and said, "Hi, fellows. My name is Bear Willis, and this is my son Eric. Which one of you is Keith?"

Instead of an answer, one of the men poked Bear in the back with his rifle, "Shut up and keep walking."

"You all sure are a friendly bunch," quipped Bear.

"I told you to shut up!"

The guard poked Bear again, but the big mountain man was ready. Bear reached around and, grabbing the rifle's barrel, yanked the gun out of the startled man's hands. At the same time, Eric charged the two men in front of him, knocking them down.

Bear leveled the rifle at the guards, "Me and my son ain't going to rob you. We just want to talk to Keith. If'n he's busy, we can come back tomorrow."

"Mister, there ain't no Keith here. Burt Blackstone owns

this property. He bought it from Keith Reeves about three months ago."

"You fellows could have saved everybody a lot of trouble if'n you had said that earlier, "said Bear.

"Maybe so, but orders are orders."

Just the two more men appeared, "That's alright, Reb," said one of the men, "Now, gents, drop that rifle and put your hands behind your back!"

Bear shrugged his shoulders. "I guess we have no choice but to do what the man says."

The men tied Bear and Eric's hands.

"WHAT IS IT YOU WANT?"

"I want you to untie our hands and point those guns somewhere else."

"I'll do that when I get some straight answers from you," said the man.

"I told you who we are," said Bear, "but you haven't told me, who you are."

"If I wanted you to know, I would have told you. Throw these two down with the other one, said the leader, "Maybe after a night in the hole, they will be more talkative."

Bear and Eric were led into the mine. One of the men lit a torch and pointed to a hole. "Grab that ladder and lower it into the hole. Then climb down."

'The hell you say," growled Bear.

"Suit yourself," said one of the men as he cocked his gun.

"Alright," said Bear, "We'll go."

Eric picked up the ladder and lowered it down the hole. Then he and Bear climbed into the hole. As soon as they reached the bottom, the ladder was pulled up. The bottom of the pit was so dark that Bear and Eric could not see their hands in front of their faces.

"In a few minutes, your eyes will adjust to the darkness," rasped a voice behind them.

"Who are you?" asked Bear.

"I'm Keith Whitehouse. The owner of this mine. Three days ago, four men broke into my cabin, tied me up, and forced me into this pit."

"What do they want?"

"They think I have discovered gold. I have, but it's just what I can get from panning. Hardly enough to kill someone over."

"Who have they killed?"

"My partner Sam Cummings. He put up a fight, and they shot him. But who are you, and what are you doing here?"

"I'm Bear Willis, and this is my son Eric. Eric and our families were part of a wagon train headed for El Paso. We met your brother, Carl, when the Texas Rangers saved our bacon. We were attacked by a band of Apache, and the Rangers showed up in the nick of time. Then the Rangers escorted us to El Paso. I talked to your brother and

mentioned that I plan to build a homestead in these mountains. He said I should stop by and meet you."

"Well, I'm sure glad you did. But sorry that you'll die
here in this miserable pit."

"So," said Eric. "I'm guessing there's no way out of this
pit except that ladder."

"Yep, we dug this hole a couple of years ago, thinking
the vein of tin ore might run through it. But when it didn't
pan out. We abandoned the pit."

"You know, Pa, we might be able to climb out of this
hole."

"Do I look like a mountain goat?" laughed Bear, "I'm too
old to be scaling up a mine shaft."

"You are," agreed Eric, "I'm not. But we need something
to cut footholds in the wall."

"We used to throw broken tools and junk down this pit.
If we got down on our hands and knees, we might find
something to dig with," said Keith. "

"Well," said Bear, as he dropped to his hands and knees,
"What are we waiting for?"

The three men felt along the floor of the pit. Bear had
almost given up when his hand touched a familiar object.

"I found an old axe head!" shouted Bear.

"Perfect," replied Eric.

Bear started chipping away at the wall, and soon he had
cut four footholds

"Give these footholds a try, son, and see if they work."

Eric stuck one foot into the notch. Then pulled himself up to the next one.

"Yeah, this will work. Hand me the axe, and I'll notch some more."

By working steadily, Eric finally reached the top of the pit. Looking around, Eric saw a length of rope, which he picked up."

"Pa, I found some rope. I'm tying one end to a timber and tossing the other to you. I figure you can tie it around your waist. Then I'll pull on the rope when you're ready to climb."

"Okay, son, throw it down."

Eric threw down the rope to Bear,

"Keith," said Bear, "You go first."

"I'm weak from not eating. So, I'm not sure I have the strength to climb out."

"Okay, I'll go. Then my son and I will haul you out."

Bear tied the rope around his waist, "Ready or not, here I come."

"I'm ready," replied Eric pulling the rope taut.

Bear climbed halfway up when his foot slipped. Eric pulled back on the rope and dug in his heels.

Fortunately, Bear was able to catch himself, "Whew, that was close," gasped Bear.

"You need to cut back on Ma's biscuits," said Eric, "I nearly slid back into the pit."

"Don't make me laugh, son."

Slowly the big mountain man made his way up and out of the hole.

"I ain't built for mountain climbing," joked Bear, "But I ain't giving up eating biscuits.

"Now, let's haul Keith up."

"Here ya go, Keith," hollered Bear, "Tie the rope around your waist and hold on."

A few minutes later, Keith Whitehouse was lying on the mine floor, exhausted but happy to be free."

"If not for you and Eric, I would have died of starvation."

"Glad we came along, "said Bear.

"I'm about hungry enough to start chewing on my boots," said Keith, "Let's go to my shack. If those outlaws haven't eaten everything, I should have enough grub to feed us."

They started to walk out of the mine when a hail of bullets drove them back.

"It's the gang that threw us into the hole," shouted Keith.

"Hey, Whitehouse! I see you made some new friends. Too bad you'll all die unless you tell us where the gold mine is."

"Damn it," yelled Keith, "I told you I don't have any gold, at least not enough to kill for. All I got was in that leather pouch."

"You're lying! That wasn't enough gold dust to fill a child's teacup."

"Maybe so," replied Keith, "but it took me three weeks to pan that much."

"You're the one who's lying, and now you and your new friends will die."

Keith slumped down behind a large rock, "I'm sorry you fellows got dragged into this."

"Weren't your fault," said Bear, "But if'n I'm going to die anyway. Is there really a gold mine?'

Keith shook his head, "Nope, on my dear Mother's grave. What I told those outlaws is the truth."

"THERE'S a creek where I get my water. One day, I noticed some glitter and decided to do some panning. I hoped maybe I'd struck it rich. I panned all up and down that creek and never found more than a few grains. Sam and I had planned to trace the stream to its source, but we never did. At the time, the tin mine was producing, and we just didn't have the time. But now even the tin has played out. I was going to sell the property, then these yahoos show up."

"I might be interested in the property," said Bear.

"First, we have to get out of here alive, Pa," commented Eric.

There is another way out of the mine," said Keith, "The mine was actually a natural cave. Sam and I blasted and removed a lot of ore. About two hundred feet into the mine, we discovered a small hole in the mine's roof. Sam was always afraid of cave-ins. So, we enlarged the hole, just large enough for a man to squeeze through."

"Show us," said Bear, "I'm getting mighty tired of being cooped up in this cave."

A shaft of light cut through the darkness, "Ha, here it is, "said Keith.

The three men crowded underneath the opening, "Are you sure we can slip through?" asked Eric.

"You and I shouldn't have a problem," replied Keith, "But your dad-------,"

"Now, you wait a minute," said Bear, "I haven't eaten in a while, so I should slide right through."

"The opening is easy to spot," said Keith, " I think it might be best to wait until the sun goes down."

Bear wiggled through the opening two hours later, "See, nothing to it."

"If you weighed a pound more, you'd never make it," said Eric as Bear popped out of the hole.

So, Pa, what's the plan?" asked Eric.

"If we wait till all the lights go out in the cabin, we should be able to catch them by surprise."

Bear, Eric, and Keith crept closer to the cabin. Through the windows, they could see the four outlaws playing cards.

"Back in the old days, remembered Bear, "We could just start shooting and wait for them to surrender. But what if you killed them," asked Eric.

"We buried them where they fell."

"How many rooms are in the cabin," asked Eric.

"There's just one room," answered Keith.

"Okay, then I suggest you and I cover the back while Pa attacks from the front.

Both Bear and Keith approved of Eric's plan."

Keith and Eric waited for Bear's signal.

They didn't have to wait long as Bear rushed forward and slammed a shoulder into the cabin's door. The door flew off its hinges and crashed into two gang members that had fallen asleep at the table. One of the men was knocked unconscious, but the other staggered to his feet, only to be grabbed by Bear and tossed through a window.

"Good God!" exclaimed Keith, "Your father is a one-man army!"

"You don't know the half of it," replied Eric, "If'n we don't want to miss all the fun, we better get in there!"

Eric pulled open the back door just as another body sailed.

"Too late," said Eric.

They walked into the cabin, and Keith shook his head in disbelief. Bear stood in the middle of the cabin. Around him were shattered chairs and the table. One outlaw was slumped in the corner, while another sat with his head between his hands.

"Gee, Pa," said Eric, "The least you could have done was leave a couple for Keith and me."

"Sorry, son, but it was hard to stop once I got started. I'll tie these two up if you and Keith take care of the other hombres."

A few minutes later, all four outlaws sat on the cabin floor. With their hands and ankles tied together. They stared at Eric, Bear, and Keith with hate-filled eyes.

"Which one of these yahoos is the leader?" asked Bear.

"The short one with the handlebar mustache," replied Keith.

"What's your name, shorty?"

"Go to hell," spat the leader.

"Fine, then, Shorty, it is," said Bear.

"I know this one," said Keith, "His name is Emanuel Lopez. I hired him a few months ago to haul ore for me. But he only worked three days, then he quit."

"The one with the scar across his right cheek is Harris, and the other is Santos. I only just met them a few days ago," pleaded Lopez.

"I bet he's the one who told the others about the gold," commented Eric.

"Yeah, but I bet there's someone else calling the shots," replied Bear.

"I agree," said Keith, "but I don't think they will talk."

"In the old days, we beat it out of them," said Bear, "But, instead, tomorrow, we'll take you to El Paso and let the sheriff decide what to do with you."

13

Bear, Eric, and Keith Whitehouse delivered the four outlaws to the local sheriff the next day. Afterward, Bear introduced Keith to his family over a late meal of tacos and beer. Bear reached for another taco when Waity slapped his hand, "Leave some for the rest of us!"

"Sorry, Luv, but these little sandwiches are tasty. What is the spice that makes me sweat?"

"They're called chilis," said Keith.

"I sure could have used these chilis when I was freezing my butt up north," chuckled Bear.

"So those four bums all have a reward on their head?" asked Sara.

"Yep, smiled Bear, "One hundred dollars each. Not bad for a few hours of work."

"Well," said Waity," You were looking for a way to earn money. Maybe hunting down outlaws and getting paid for it is something you could do."

"Nah, Eric and I have a better idea? Why don't you tell them, son?"

"Keith told us that he's ready to sell his land. Now the tin mine is about played out, and there's not enough gold to fill a tooth. However, there's a valley on the property. Keith tells us it's a perfect spot for a small farm. Isn't that right, Keith?"

"Yes, the valley is tucked between two ridges. They're about thirty acres, with a small stream running through it. The best way I can describe the valley is that it's like a piece of paradise tucked up in the Franklin Mountains. There's only one thing."

"Oh, here we go," laughed Waity, "I should have known. So, what is this one thing?"

"We share the water rights with some neighbors?"

"Neighbors?" questioned Bear, "I thought you said the land was remote. It's a wild, untamed wilderness, you said. But now you're telling me we have neighbors!"

They are called Yaquis," said Keith. "Their tribal land is originally south of the Rio Grande. But centuries ago, the Spanish came and tried to push them north. But the Yaquis fought back. The Spanish never defeated them, and neither have the Mexicans. Tired of fighting, a small group of Yaquis moved into the Franklin Mountains."

"When I bought the land. I didn't know the Yaquis lived

nearby or that they had water rights to the creek. I was afraid I would have to fight them over that creek. But when I met them, their chief assured me they were peaceful people. They respected my right to the valley, and I respected their ancestral right to the water. I think you'll find them to be good neighbors."

Waity smiled, "I know that when my husband gets an idea in his thick skull, he's like a racehorse with the bit in his mouth. I will agree to the land deal, but first, I want to meet these Yaquis."

"I'd be happy to introduce you," agreed Keith.

"Good, then it's settled. We'll leave tomorrow," said Bear.

Waity laughed, "See what I mean about a horse with a bit?"

They all laughed at Waity's comment. All except Bear, who pretended his feelings were hurt.

KEITH WHITEHOUSE escorted BEAR, Eric, and their families to the Franklin Mountains the next day. Bear was excited about starting a new chapter. He was confident that his time in the mountains and living amongst the Shoshone and other tribes would bode him well with the Yaquis.

"Whoa!" said Bear pulling at the reins, "Well, Luv, there's our valley."

Stretched out below was a green valley sandwiched

between the tans and grays of the mountains.

"It takes my breath away," smiled Waity, "I just hope the Yaquis welcome us."

"I think they will, especially when they get to know you, Sara, and the children. But first, let's set up camp by our little creek."

"It isn't ours yet, Bear."

"I know, but it will be."

"I told you it was like paradise," said Keith as he rode up to the wagon.

"I can't believe a valley like this could exist up here in the mountains," said Waity.

"I think it is because of the creek. This little trickle of water has never run dry. Nearly every stream in the Franklin Mountains dries up come summer. But not this creek. Of course, the Yaquis have a different tale."

"What's that," asked Waity.

"They believe a Yaquis princess was so heartbroken over the death of her lover that she wept for forty days, flooding the valley. When she finally stopped crying. The tears formed this stream."

"I like that story better," said Waity, "What is the name of the creek?"

"I can't pronounce the Yaquis' name, but it's called Princess's Lament in English."

"That's too sad a name. The children and I will come up with a better one."

"Speaking of the Yaquis," said Bear, "When will we meet

them?"

"Tomorrow, we'll ride out to their village," answered Keith and bring the children."

"Why?" asked Waity.

"Because it'll show the Yaquis that you come in peace. Also, we should bring them some fresh meat. Bear, how good are you with that rifle?"

"Ha, Sara's a better shot," laughed Waity.

"It's true," acknowledged Bear, "My daughter-in-law can flick a flea off a buffalo's hump at two hundred paces."

"Okay," chuckled Keith, "Remind me to never mess with your family."

"Yep," said Bear, "that wouldn't be wise."

"So, what do you want me to shoot?" asked Sara.

"There's peccary in the valley. They're active in the evening. If Sara can shoot one, we'll give it to the Yaquis."

"Okay," said Sara.

"I'll show you a good spot to set up," said Keith, "The peccary are skittish critters. The slightest noise and they'll skedaddle."

BEAR and his family made camp, and after eating their evening meal, Keith Whitehouse led Eric and Sara across the valley to a cluster of rocks.

"The peccary's favorite food is acorns," explained

Whitehouse, and that tree line is loaded with oak trees. Sara and Eric began climbing up the rocks when Keith stopped them.

"Watch out for snakes," warned Keith as he poked around the rocks with a stick. Suddenly there was a rattle, and a rattlesnake slithered out of a hole. Keith pinned the snake's head down with the stick. Then drawing his knife chopped off its head.

"Another gift," Keith said as he held up the twitching headless snake. "The meat is tasty, and the snake skin is used for decorating their clothing."

"Sara got into position behind a rock. She placed her rifle on the top of the rock and waited. They did not have to wait long before three peccary emerged from the woods. Sara could hear them grunting as the animals rooted around for the acorns.

"Sara," whispered Keith, "take the female to the right of the big boar. Her meat will be nice and tender."

Sara nodded her head and concentrated on the shot. The woods echoed with the roar of the rifle shot.

"You got her," exclaimed Eric, "Nice shot."

The peccary ran a few feet before falling down. "Okay, let's go and get your first kill."

Waity, Eric, and Keith approached the downed peccary. Suddenly they heard a grunt and turned as a big boar charged from the woods.

Before they could react, a figure raced up to the peccary

and thrust his lance into the animals' side. The boar squealed and took three more steps before falling over. The Yaquis pulled out his spear and said, "That was a good shot."

"Thank you," replied Sara, "But if it wasn't for you and your spear, that peccary would have caused some damage."

"I was tracking the peccary, hoping to kill one, when I heard the rifle shot. I have never seen a woman shoot like a man."

"Thank you, but I like to think I shoot better than most men."

The Yaquis smiled then, turning to Keith, spoke to him in Yaquis.

"Keith nodded and said something in Yaquis."

Sara, Eric," said Keith, "This is Juan Leyva of the Yaquis. Juan is the son of their chief. Juan, this is Sara and Eric Willis. They are the folks who are buying my land. We plan to visit your father tomorrow."

"Welcome to our valley. I hope you'll be welcome here. I will tell my father to expect you. We have a feast in your honor."

Juan quickly gutted the peccary and, lifting it to his shoulder, walked back into the woods.

"Mr. Whitehouse, do you care to share in the joke?'

"I'm sorry, Sara, I'm not sure what you mean?"

"Juan spoke to you in his language, and you both enjoyed a laugh. I hope it wasn't at my expense."

"Oh, I can assure you, Sara, that we weren't making fun

of you. Juan said you were an unusual woman, and I said wait till he sees the rest of the family."

"I guess I'll take that as a compliment," smiled Sara.

"If you two are through," interrupted Eric, "We should get this peccary back to camp before we attract the wolves."

14

Hurry, children," called Waity, "We don't want to keep the Yaquis waiting."

"Mama! Charlie pulled the ribbon out of my hair!"

"Charlie. Hand me that ribbon, and if you don't behave, I'll make you wear a ribbon for a week!"

Charlie approached Waity with his head bent down. "I'm sorry, Ma. I was only trying to straighten it."

"Charlie, do you know what's worse than teasing your sister?" asked Bear.

"No, Pa,"

"It's lying about it! Now no more teasing!"

"Yes, Pa,"

The Yaquis village was five miles from their campsite, so Bear and Eric decided to travel in the wagon. Keith

Whitehouse rode his horse, and the two Irish Wolfhounds trotted beside the wagon.

The weather was fair, with a few clouds sprinkled across the blue sky.

"I swear," said Waity, "I don't think I ever saw a sky so blue."

"It's right, pretty country," agreed Bear.

"I hope the Yaquis are as welcoming as Keith Whitehouse says they are."

"From what Eric and Sara said about the chief's son, they're peaceful."

"People talked about forcing the Yaquis off the land and driving them back to Mexico."

"Yep, I heard the same thing," replied Bear, "It seems someone has been stealing cattle, and of course, folks are blaming the Yaquis."

"Maybe we can find out who's really taking the cattle."

"Waity, we just got here. Let's get settled first before we get involved in catching cattle rustlers. Let's leave that to the Texas Rangers."

"You're right. We have enough to keep ourselves busy without chasing outlaws."

Their arrival at the Yaquis village caused quite a stir. The tribe was expecting a family of homesteaders. So, they were surprised to see two huge dogs running alongside the wagon. Then when Bear stepped down from the wagon and stretched the kinks out of his six-foot-six-inch frame, the much shorter Yaquis stared. Mothers shooed their children into the huts for fear the giant wolfhounds would attack and eat them, and the men stood protectively by their wives.

An older man, followed by Juan and three warriors, approached them.

"Let me do all the talking," said Keith.

"I thought they were expecting us?' said Bear.

"They were, but I should have warned them about you, your family, and those hounds."

"What is the Yaquis' word for peace be with you?"

Keith thought for a moment, then spoke the words slowly.

Bear turned to the Chief and repeated the words as best he could."

The older man's face crinkled into a smile while several men and women covered their mouths to stifle a laugh."

BEAR SHOT KEITH A PUZZLED LOOK, "What so funny?"

"You said I have many fleas."

Waity was the first to laugh, then the children, followed by Bear's rumble.

"Well, that broke the ice," said Waity. "Maybe, you can have the hounds do a few tricks."

Bear called the hounds to him and, using his hands, gave the command to sit. Thor and Odin sat before Bear, waiting for their next command. Bear waved his hand in a circle, and immediately, the dogs began jumping over each other.

By now, the children had joined the adults, clapped their hands, and laughed as Bear put Thor and Odin through a series of tricks. Finally, the hounds returned to Bear's side and sat on their haunches.

"Tell the Yaquis that the children can pet the hounds."

Keith repeated what Bear had said. The children were hesitant to approach the hounds. But once a couple of the children stepped forward and petted Thor and Odin, more soon followed. Soon, the hounds were surrounded by giggling children.

Keith Whitehouse made the proper introductions.

LATER AFTER A MEAL of roasted peccary and tamales filled with a fiery corn and bean mixture: Bear, Eric, and Keith sat with Chief Leyva outside the chief's hut and smoked their pipes and talked.

Chief Leyva spoke Spanish and a few words of English. So, with Keith acting as an interpreter, Bear and Chief Leyva discussed various topics, from family to the northern tribes and some of Bear's adventures. Finally, the talk turned serious.

"Chief Leyva is worried about the future. He fears they will be driven from this land like they were from Mexico," said Keith.

"Tell Chief Leyva that as long as I have breath in me, my family and I will stand with his people."

Whitehouse, speaking in Spanish, repeated what Bear had said. The Chief nodded in Bear's direction and, looking the mountain man in the eye, said in halting English, "White man promises, then break promise."

"Sadly, that is true, but as you'll soon find out, I'm not like most white men."

Bear pulled off the necklace his first wife, Little Sparrow, had made for him and handed it to Chief Leyva.

"Many moons ago, I survived a long cold northern winter by sheltering in a bear's den. My wife made this necklace using bear claws to remind me of my ordeal. I have never taken it off until now. I give it to you as a token of my friendship and to seal my promise."

Bear could tell that Chief Leyva was moved by Bear's gift. The Yaquis chief nodded and, looking at Bear, spoke in his native tongue.

"You've just made a friend," said Keith, "The chief thanks you for the gift. He would also like to offer a gift to you as a symbol of friendship."

Chief Leyva spoke to his son, who quickly left. In a few minutes, Juan returned with a black stallion. Juan walked over to a speechless Bear and handed him the reins.

"Bear ran his hand down the horse's neck and over the animal's withers, "A fine animal, thank you, Chief Leyva."

. . .

"You made quite an impression on the Yaquis," said Keith as Bear and his family returned to the homestead.

"Leyva is a good man; his small band has suffered greatly. They deserve to be left in peace."

"I don't think that's possible," replied Keith, "The Yaquis are caught between the Mexicans and the Texans. They have nowhere to go. So, I'm afraid that sooner or later, sparks will fly."

"I made a pledge to the chief, and I will stand with the Yaquis."

"That's something that maybe tested," cautioned Keith, "I'm sure you've heard the talk accusing the Yaquis of stealing cattle?"

"I have. Do you think anything will come of it?"

"Who knows," shrugged Keith, "Except for you and I, the Yaquis don't have many friends, and there's always a few hotheads who might decide to take the law into their own hands."

"What about the sheriff?" asked Bear.

"That old fart," laughed Keith, "He's useless in a gunfight. They just keep him around to collect taxes. His deputy Bart McGrew does most of the work. Besides, the sheriff's jurisdiction ends at the town line."

"What about the Rangers?"

"Yeah, they're the Yaquis' best bet, but the Rangers have a lot of territory to cover. By the time word gets to them, and they ride all night, the Yaquis could be buzzard bait."

"So, we're on our own?" asked Bear.

"Yep, that's about the size of it," replied Whitehouse.

"Being on our own is nothing new," replied Bear.

Keith laughed, "I'd like to stay around and help, but I think you can handle anything that comes your way. Besides, it won't be long before the folks around El Paso will know that Bear Willis and his family are not to be messed with."

15

Bart McGrew spat a wad of tobacco, "Is that the one who hauled in Lopez and the others?"

Clay 'Shotgun' Rogers lifted the brim of his hat, "Calls himself Bear Willis. Keith Whitehouse sold him that patch of land he owned up in the Franklins."

"He sure is a tall drink of water," said McGrew, "And look at the size of his dogs. I ain't never seen hounds that big."

"They're called Irish Wolfhounds. I was told the Irish bred the dogs to hunt wolves," answered Rogers.

"No kidding? How come you know so much about the man?"

"I keep my mouth shut and my ears open," said Rogers.

"Well, they ruined my plans. So, now I'll have to deal with them myself."

"Do you think Lopez and his men will spill the beans and tell Sheriff Jones that you're the one who hired them?"

"Not if they want to live," snarled McGrew, "Remember, I'm the deputy sheriff, and Sheriff Jones has to go to Austin tomorrow, so that puts me in charge."

"Yep, being a deputy has its advantages," admitted Rogers.

"Let's go over and have a chat with this tall drink of water," suggested McGrew.

"Sure, why not? It is the neighborly thing to do."

McGrew and Rogers strutted over to where Bear was loading his wagon.

"You Bear Willis?" asked McGrew.

"I am," answered Bear, "What can I do for you?

"I'm Bart McGrew, the town's deputy sheriff. It's my job to know about newcomers and ensure you don't cause any trouble."

"Hmm, so you're sort of like the town's busybody? Ain't that something old women usually do?"

"Are you trying to be smart, Willis?" asked McGrew.

"Nope, just trying to figure you out. If'n you are the deputy, then you should know that we delivered some hombres to your jail."

Caught off guard, McGrew paused, "Of course, I knew that. I just wanted to introduce myself."

"Well, you've done that," replied Bear, "Now, if'n you don't mind, I have to load this wagon and get back to my homestead before dark."

"You better watch your mouth, big man," interrupted Rogers.

"And why's that?"

"Folks around here don't take kindly to strangers siding with the Yaquis."

"I never said anything about the Yaquis," replied Bear.

"Ah, Sheriff Jones told us," replied Rogers.

Bear stared at the man for a long time, "Must be hot wearing that long black coat. Whatya hiding under there?"

"What I wear ain't none of your concerned," snapped Rogers.

"Excuse me, you're right. As far as I'm concerned, you can wear a lady's dress and put rouge on your cheeks."

"Why, I ought to!"

"Calm down, Rogers," warned McGrew, "This ain't the time or place."

The deputy sheriff put his hand on Bear's chest. Thor and Odin, quietly sitting at Bear's side, stood and growled as the hairs on their backs stood straight up.

"If'n I was you, I remove my hand," snarled Bear.

McGrew looked at the hounds and lowered his hand, "If you ever again threaten me with those beasts, I'll shoot them and nail the hides to my barn."

"I don't make threats, deputy. I make promises, and I always keep my promises. Now am I free to go?" Bear asked as he glared at the smaller man. Finally, McGrew stepped aside.

. . .

"I THOUGHT he was going to sic the hounds on you," said Shotgun Rogers.

"If he did, I figured you would blast Willis with your shotgun, and I'd plug those hounds."

"Maybe I ought to pay Willis a visit."

"Yeah, okay, we'll ride out and see what he's up to," agreed McGrew.

Bear went about his business and noticed that most people stared angrily at him or turned away. Finally, he climbed into his wagon and rode out of town.

Arriving back at his campsite, Bear was unloading his wagon when Eric walked over, "Something happened in town?"

"What makes you think that," asked Bear as he tossed a keg of nails on the ground.

"I know you, Pa; something got under your skin."

"Your right. I ran into a little weasel. A deputy sheriff named Bart McGrew. He warned me about befriending the Yaquis. I'm afraid we haven't seen the last of him."

"What are we going to do?" asked Eric.

"We're going to build our homestead, stay true to our friends, and stay alert for anyone who wishes to harm us or the Yaquis."

"Alright, Pa, now let's get this wagon unloaded."

THE NEXT DAY, Bear awoke to the sounds of wagon wheels and the braying of mules. Bear rolled over and grabbed his gun. Waity rubbed her eyes, "What's going on?" asked Waity.

"I have no idea," said Bear as he lifted the tent flap.

Bear couldn't believe his eyes. Emerging from the woods were two wagons loaded with timber. Several Yaquis men, women, and their children walked beside the wagons. On their backs were baskets filled with food. Leading the group were Chief Leyva and his son Juan.

"Chief Leyva, what are you doing here?" asked Bear.

"We come to build your home," said Leyva.

Bear and Waity looked at the wagons and all the food, "Really, Chief, this is all too much."

"It has been a good year," explained the chief, "The Great Spirit has blessed us with abundant rain and a good harvest. We wish to share our abundance with our new neighbors and build a house for you."

Leyva waved his hand, and men began unloading the wood, "Where do you want your house?" asked Juan.

"OVER THERE, by that grove of trees."

"An excellent choice," replied Juan. He called to his men, and they started piling the timber near the trees.

For the next three days, Bear, Eric, and the rest of the family worked alongside the Yaquis. Each night they ate together. The women shared their recipes with Waity, who couldn't get enough of the spicy food.

"White man's food is plain and tasteless compared to Mexican," she explained as she made another tortilla.

ON THE LAST NIGHT, the Yaquis and Bear's family feasted on venison and peccary. As the meal ended, Bear stood and addressed the gathering, "My family and I can't thank you enough for your kindness and generosity. Because of you, our house is nearly completed. The garden is planted, and our well is dug. Chief Leyva, we couldn't have done all this without you. During our time together, we have gotten to know your people. I hope this is the start of a long and valued friendship. If there is anything you need, do not hesitate to ask."

Chief Leyva stood, and the two men shook hands.

The following morning the Yaquis returned to their village.

"WHAT DID I TELL YOU?" hissed Shotgun Rogers.

"You were right," replied Bart McGrew, "That Indian lover Willis is a danger. Soon more Yaquis will move into the mountains. We must act now before this gets out of hand,"

The two men crawled down the hill, mounted their horses, and rode back to town.

· · ·

"I'M GOING into town tomorrow, said Bear, "We need hinges for the doors and another box of nails."

"Don't forget my weather vane," replied Waity, "The blacksmith said he'd have it ready by now."

"Okay, anything else?"

"Licorice," shouted Charlie and Jed.

"And peppermint sticks," added Rose, "Remember you said if we weeded the garden, you would buy us peppermint sticks."

Bear laughed, "Yes, I remember."

"I could use about four yards of red checkered gingham cloth and black thread."

"You better write me a list. My memory ain't what it used to be."

An hour later, with his shopping list safely tucked in his shirt, Bear climbed into his wagon. As soon as he sat down, Thor jumped up beside him.

"Okay, big fella, you can come, but this time behave yourself."

The Irish Wolfhound responded by thumping its tail on the wagon's wooden sideboard.

"It's a good thing Eric went hunting with Odin. I don't think I can handle the two of you and shop at the same time."

Each time the hounds accompanied Bear into El Paso, they caused a stir as most folks had never seen a wolfhound. Worse were the children who clustered around the hounds. Thor and Odin adored the attention, but Bear wanted to make a quick trip and return home before sunset.

BEAR'S first stop was Whitney's Mercantile. From the moment Bear stepped into the busy store, he knew something wasn't right. The last time he was in the store Sam Whitney and his wife, Emma, had greeted him warmly. But now they did their best to ignore him. The other customers also gave Bear the cold shoulder. He had enough after waiting several minutes and seeing the Whitneys wait on customers instead of him.

"What do I have to do to get some service?"

At the sound of his voice, two women, standing at the counter, chatting with the Whitneys, quickly gathered their things and left the store.

"You needn't shout, Mr. Willis. We will take care of you shortly," huffed Mrs. Whitney.

"I was patiently waiting my turn, but then you waited on customers that came into the store after I did," explained Bear.

"You're lucky we even allow you into the store," snapped Mr. Whitney.

"What, why?" snarled Bear.

The Whitneys stepped back from the counter, fearful of the big mountain man.

"We don't service Indian lovers. That's why," stuttered a nervous Mr. Whitney.

"Oh, that's it! Then I'll just help myself."

Before the Whitneys could object, Bear opened a jar of licorice sticks and removed six pieces. Then he did the same with the penny candy, next Bear walked behind the counter and took down a bolt of red gingham cloth. Taking it to the counter, Bear unrolled the fabric and cut the gingham to length. Next, he carefully placed the material back on the shelf.

"Where do you hide the needles?"

"Ah, in the middle drawer under the fabric."

"Bear selected four needles and placed them on the counter with his other items. By now, several people had gathered, eager to see what the mountain man would do next.

"Okay," said Bear, "That should do it, and add the cost of a keg of nails. I'll pick them up from your barn when I leave. Now, how much do I owe you?"

"Well. I never!" scoffed Mrs. Whitney, crossing her arms and stomping into the back room.

Bear glared at Mr. Whitney, "How much?"

"Ah, that'll be two dollars and ninety-five cents.'

Bear tossed three silver dollars on the counter, "Keep the change!"

Finally, Bear gathered his things and walked out the door.

His next stop was the blacksmith shop. Ralph, the town blacksmith, greeted Bear with a hearty "Howdy,"

"Well, that's a better welcome than I got at Whitney's," said Bear.

"The town folks have been warned to stay away from you and your family," explained Ralph.

"This is because I'm an Indian lover?"

"Yep,"

"But what about you?"

"To hell with McGrew. Nobody tells me who I can or cannot do business with. McGrew is always trying to get folks to drive the Yaquis out of the mountains. He claims that allowing the Yaquis to stay will only attract more Indians. Some folks had a family member killed or wounded by the Indians, so no love is lost for anyone who befriends the Yaquis."

"I see. Well, that's too bad 'cause I ain't going anywhere, and neither are the Yaquis."

"GOOD FOR YOU!" replied the blacksmith., "But don't think everyone hates the Yaquis. The trouble is most folks are afraid of McGrew. Everyone knows that if you cross him, he will kill you."

"But you're not?'

The blacksmith laughed, "I'm the only smithy for miles around. Besides, I mind my business, and they leave me alone."

"Well, I appreciate your honesty and advice," said Bear shaking the man's hand.

. . .

BEAR LOADED HIS WAGON, unaware that he was being watched.

"The best place to bushwack Willis is where the trail narrows. You know, the place about five miles out of town, where that rockslide nearly blocked the road?"

"Yep, I do,"

"You taking any of the cowboys?" asked McGrew.

"Nope, they're all out gathering up cattle. Besides, no need to have witnesses if you're going to murder someone," replied Shotgun.

McGrew smiled, "No. I reckon not."

"This shouldn't take long," said Rogers mounting his horse, "I'll meet you at the Silver Dollar Cantina in a couple of hours."

"Good luck," said McGrew as Rogers rode away.

16

The hot sun and the swaying wagon made Bear drowsy. He was nearing the rockslide when Thor growled. Instantly Bear was on guard, "What's the matter, Thor? You smell a bunny rabbit."

Just then, Bear caught movement behind the rocks. He pulled his gun and urged his mules forward when a shotgun blast peppered his wagon. Thor yelped, and Bear cursed as pellets hit him in the leg. Bear grunted in pain and rolled out of the wagon. His attacker, thinking he had mortally wounded Bear, slowly crept closer and closer. Beside Bear, Thor growled as blood trickled down his chest.

"Stay, Thor," commanded Bear, "You're wounded.

Then ignoring the pain in his thigh, Bear peeked over the wagon bed. Seeing the outlaw emerge from behind the rocks, Bear fired, hitting his attacker twice in the chest. Bear waited to see if he had killed the man. Then hearing nothing, Bear focused his attention on Thor.

Bear probed the spot high on Thor's chest. Each time Bear touched the area, Thor whimpered. Then with a jerk, Bear removed a sliver of wood.

"It was just a flesh wound, you big baby. When we get home, I'll have Waity wash you, and you'll be good to go."

Unfortunately, Bear's gunshot wounds were more serious. He had been hit five times in the right upper thigh. Two of the pellets were lodged just under the skin. But the other three were deeper. Bear removed his bandana and wrapped his thigh tightly. Then he helped Thor into the wagon, and together they headed home.

"Here comes, Pa," shouted Rose to her brothers.

The three children were helping Waity weed the garden. But at the sight of the wagon, they dropped their hoes and ran to meet Bear.

Waity laughed as the children raced each other down the path. When Bear suggested they move south, Waity was uncertain it was the right thing to do. But now, with the growing friendship between the family, the Yaquis, and this beautiful valley, Waity was sure it was worth the trip.

But, Waity's pleasant thoughts were suddenly shattered when she heard Rose yell, "Mama, somethings wrong with Papa!"

Waity hiked up her dress and ran toward the wagon. As she ran, Waity noticed that the wagon was wobbling from one side of the trail to the other. Her heart skipped when she saw Bear slumped over and Thor resting his head on Bear's broad back.

"Bear," she screamed as she flew by her children, "Charlie find Eric and Sara. Tell them to hurry!"

"Whoa," said Waity as she grabbed the mules' harnesses. The wagon ground to a stop, "Jed, Rose, keep the mules still."

Thor lifted his head and whined as Waity climbed into the wagon. She placed a hand on Bear's back and, feeling him take a breath, said, "I'm here, Luv. Can you sit up?"

Bear moaned and mumbled, "Yes,"

"Okay, let me help."

BEAR SIGHED as Waity helped him into a sitting position, "My leg, shot, too much blood."

Waity looked at his leg and gasped. Bear's pant leg was soaked with blood.

"Hang on, I need to get you to the cabin."

"Rose, Jed, climb in the back."

When the children were in the wagon, Waity snapped the reins and yelled, "Giddy-up,"

The mules picked up the pace, and soon they arrived at the cabin. As they did, Eric and Sara came running around the corner of the house.

"What happened?" asked Eric.

"All I know is that your father's been shot in the leg and has lost a lot of blood. We need to move him inside, so I can see the damage."

They started to help Bear down when he stopped and said, "Thor, hurt,"

Eric looked at Thor's blood-stained chest and said, "Easy, Thor, we'll come back for you once we get Pa settled."

The big Irish Wolfhound seemed to understand as he lowered his head, resting it upon his paws.

Bear groaned as they laid him on the plank table. Waity took a small knife and slit Bear's pant leg. Waity breathed a sigh of relief as she looked at the wound, "Buckshot,"

"I count five pellets, "said Eric, "Two are just under the skin, but the other three are deep. We'll have to dig them out. Before the buckshot poisons the leg."

"Whiskey," croaked Bear, "Then dig."

Waity looked at Eric, who nodded, "Sara, please take the children to our camp. Maybe you can bake some ginger cookies."

"Come along, children. Your Pa will be okay."

"Can we bring Pa some cookies?" asked Rose.

"Of course, dear," replied Sara. "I'm sure he'll like that."

"Lift your head, Pa. Here's the whiskey."

Eric lifted Bear's head while Waity held the jug to his lips. Bear swallowed the whiskey and coughed, "More,"

Waity let Bear drink until; he finally pushed the jug

away. While Bear drank, Waity tore a white petticoat into long strips. Finally, all was ready. Waity gave Bear a piece of leather to bite down on. Bear nodded his head, and Eric started cutting. Beads of sweat popped out on Bear's head, and a couple of times, he grunted as Eric removed one pellet after another. Finally, it was over. In a tin plate were the five pellets of buckshot. Waity had stitched up the holes and then wrapped the wounds tightly.

After soaking it in cool water, she took a cloth and mopped her husband's head.

"It's over, Luv. Rest now."

Bear took Waity's hand, "How's Thor?"

Waity smiled, "Oh, he's okay. His thick hair stopped the piece of wood from causing any real damage."

"That's good to hear," said Bear, "I sure wish I had Thor's hide."

Waity and Eric laughed, "If you did, I don't think I would have married you. You're hairy enough as it is."

"So, Pa," interrupted Eric, "What happened?"

"You know where the trail narrows?"

"Yeah," said Eric.

"Well, someone was hiding behind a rock. When I rode past, he popped up and took a shot at me?"

"Why did he use a shotgun instead of a rifle?" asked Eric.

"Heck, if I know," replied Bear, "Wait a minute! When I talked to that deputy sheriff, Bart McGrew, there was a hombre with him who called himself Shotgun Rogers. He wore a long black coat, just like the shooters."

"Any idea why Robers would want you killed," asked Waity.

"Rogers' works for Deputy Sheriff McGrew. The weasel gave me a hard time when I was in town. He called me an Indian lover. I didn't pay much attention to McGrew, but maybe I should have."

"You can't change the past, Luv," said Waity, "All we can do is move forward or die."

"So that's why he tried to kill you?"

"It's the only thing that makes sense," said Bear.

"How dangerous is McGrew?" asked Eric.

"According to the blacksmith, McGrew has killed anyone questioning his authority. McGrew believes there's gold on our land. That has to be why he has it in for us and wants the Yaquis to leave. "It's like we're a threat because of our friendship with the Yaquis."

"So, what do we do?" asked Waity.

"Just keep doing what we've been doing. We have a homestead to build. The cabins and barns need to be finished, and the gardens tended. However, we need to keep the children close. Carry a gun everywhere you go and keep your eyes open. Let Thor and Odin run free; they're our best guards," said Bear.

"Okay, but you're going to take it easy. Those wounds need to heal, and your body has to replace all that blood you lost."

Bear just smiled, "Yes, dear,"

A COUPLE DAYS LATER, despite Waity's concerns, Bear was up and doing light work. Today, he and Eric were riding over to the Yaquis village.

"Bear, Eric, it is good to see you have recovered," said Chief Juan Leyva.

"How did you know I was shot?" asked Bear.

Leyva smiled, "There is little that happens in the valley that I don't know about."

"I'm concerned," said Bear, "I believe Bart McGrew is behind the shooting and that he'll try again."

"Yes," agreed the chief, "McGrew is a man not to be trusted."

"Then we better keep our guns handy," replied Bear.

"That would be the wise thing to do," agreed Chief Leyva.

17

W hat the hell happened to you?" asked Burt McGrew.

Shotgun Rogers had just limped into the El Paso jailhouse with his head wrapped in a bloody white bandage.

"Bear Willis, that's what happened," snarled Shotgun, "and his big dog."

"Did you ambush him where the trail narrows?"

"Yep,"

Then why do I get the feeling that Bear Willis is still alive?"

"Because he is," admitted Rogers.

"So, what happened?

"Well, I set up just where you told me. I wasn't there for

ten minutes when Willis and his dog rode up in their wagon. I fired, hitting Willis and the dog."

"I thought I had killed the mountain man, so I went to look. That's when he shot me. The bullets knocked me back, and I hit my head on a rock. When I came to, Willis and his hound were gone. That mountain man is one tough hombre."

"The bastard is still alive!" exploded McGrew, "Now we have to devise another way of killing him." McGrew thought for a moment, "Willis has a family, a wife, and three young'uns. That's his weak link. So, we kidnap one of his rug rats and use the brat as bait."

"That could work," commented Rogers.

"I wasn't asking for you're okay," snapped McGrew.

"Sorry," replied Rogers, "Just trying to be helpful."

"Yeah, well, don't. When are the cowboys due back?"

"In two or three days," replied Rogers.

"Okay, listen, those yahoos will want to get drunk. But tell them I'll pay each man twenty dollars instead of the usual ten if he puts off drinking and joins us."

"Alright, Bart, I will," agreed Rogers.

SHOTGUN ROGERS SLID into a chair at Emma's Cantina five days later.

"Well," said McGrew, "Those boys have been in town two days."

"Yep, but you know cowboys. I couldn't get them to give up a night on the town. But now most are broke."

"Okay, but I'll only pay them ten dollars."

"Well, here's the thing, they want twenty."

"Twenty!" shouted McGrew.

"That's the deal."

McGrew swore but then said, Okay, twenty, but it has to be tonight. Tell the boys to meet us at midnight at the barn."

McGrew pulled out his pocket watch, "Twelve-thirty, where the hell are they?"

A few minutes later, the cowboys and Shotgun Rogers arrived. Several men were drunk and barely able to stay in their saddles.

"How many?" asked McGrew.

"I was able to round up ten men," said Shotgun Rogers.

"Ten! and half of them are drunk! I can't use drunk men. Give them a dollar and send them on their way."

"But that'll leave us with five," protested Rogers.

"I can count, you idiot! I rather have five sober men than a bunch of drunks."

McGrew, Rogers, and the five sober cowboys headed out of El Paso an hour later. The blacksmith was on his way to his shop. He had a large order to fill and needed to get his forge fired up.

"*What the devil is McGrew up to now,*" he wondered.

The smithy shrugged his shoulders and entered his shop. After starting the forge, he set a pot of coffee on the wood stove and sat down to wait for the coffee to brew. By dawn, he was fast at work until Kit Carson pulled up outside the blacksmith shop."

"Ralph," said Kit as he walked into the shop. "You're up early."

"Yep, got a big job and thought I get a jump on it."

"Well, I'm glad you are. My horse threw a shoe."

"I can't do it today, but I should be able to shoe him tomorrow."

"That'll work. By the way, I saw McGrew and a bunch of cowboys leaving town. Do you have any idea where there were going?"

"I'm not sure, but one of the men said McGrew plans to teach newcomers a lesson."

"Newcomers?" asked Carson, "that could only be Willis and his family."

The blacksmith nodded, "Yep, that was my conclusion. For years, McGrew has used his deputy sheriff's badge to intimidate folks and fatten his wallet. I met Bear Willis. He seems an honest man and not one I would want to mess with."

"You're right there," agreed Kit, "Bear and I guided a wagon train from California to El Paso. He's the toughest, roughest man I've ever met. Fearless in battle and a trusted friend. If McGrew thinks he can scare off Bear Willis, he has another thought coming. You know what happens when you poke a Bear?"

"Yep, I do."

"Well, McGrew is about to poke Bear Willis, and God help him when he does!"

"But what can we do?"

"I need a fast horse. That black stallion in the corral should do."

"He's half-wild, Kit. I traded a Yaquis for the stallion and haven't had time to work with him."

"A Yaquis, eh, Good. I'm half-wild myself, so we should get along."

Kit unsaddled his horse and carried the gear over to the corral. He set the saddle on a fence rail and watched as the stallion snorted and pranced around the corral.

"He's full of spit and vinegar," said Carson.

"Yep, he knows something is up," replied Ralph.

"What's his name?"

"THUNDER," replied the blacksmith, and if you can get that saddle on him, you'll know why he's called that."

"Thunder, eh, well Thunder, do you want to take a ride?"

Kit climbed over the corral fence, then taking his horse blanket and bridle, ambled over to Thunder. As he approached the stallion, Kit began speaking softly in Yaquis. At first, Thunder snorted and backed up against the fence. But Kit kept whispering to the horse, allowing Thunder to settle down. Ralph couldn't believe his eyes as Kit began stoking the stallion's neck. The Kit placed the bridle over Thunder's neck. Next, he laid the blanket over Thunder. Finally, he led the stallion over to the gate.

"Ain't ya going to put a saddle on him?"

"Nope, he was raised by Yaquis, and they don't use a saddle, just a blanket."

Kit swung onto Thunder's back. "Easy, big fellow, everything will be alright."

The stallion reared its head but remained still. That's a boy. Easy does it. Hand me my rifle, open the gate, and step back."

Ralph handed Kit the rifle, which Carson slung over his shoulders. "Okay," said Carson, "Now, the gate."

As soon as the blacksmith opened the gate, the stallion bolted out. The last the blacksmith saw of Thunder, Carson was hanging on for dear life as the stallion raced down the deserted street."

CHIEF LEYVA LOOKED up as Kit riding a black stallion, rode into the village. Kit pulled at the reins, and Thunder blowing through his nose halted.

The Yaquis chief smiled, "The great Kit Carson, it is

good to see you, my friend, and you're riding my son's stallion."

Kit dismounted, "Your son has a good eye for horse flesh."

"Come, we will eat, smoke, and you can tell me of your latest adventure."

"I would like nothing more. But the reason I'm here is to ask for your help. I believe McGrew and six hombres plan to drive Bear Willis and his family from the valley."

"McGrew that piece of dog dung!"

"Yep, I agree. I'm here because I need some of your warriors."

"Yes, of course," replied Leyva. Then the chief waved his hand, summoning a young boy. Fetch my son," ordered Chief Leyva. The boy ran off. A few minutes later, Juan approached.

"Kit, you are riding the stallion I traded to the black-smith. Have you come to trade it back to me?"

"It is a fine animal," said Kit," but I just borrowed it. The reason I'm here is I need your help. Bear Willis and his family are in danger. McGrew and six men rode out of El Paso last night. I fear they will attack Willis, drive him out of the valley, or kill Bear and his family."

"Then we must hurry!" replied Juan, "I will gather my men."

Ten minutes later, Kit and the Yaquis galloped out of the village.

18

Bear and Eric were up early. They had planned to pull tree stumps to make way for a cornfield. They had just hitched up the mules when Odin began to growl, then Thor, who was playing with Charlie, raced to the split rail fence and started barking. Then both hounds ran in the direction of the ridge.

"Trouble," said Eric.

"Yep, Charlie, run and tell your Ma to stay inside. Then warn Aunt Sara."

"Yes, Pa," shouted Charlie as he raced to the cabin.

"Thor, Odin, heel!" Instantly, the Irish Wolfhounds stopped. They stared at the ridgeline and whined. For a second, Bear feared the hounds would disobey his command, but then they turned and raced back to Bear.

"Good dogs," said Bear, rubbing Thor and Odin's heads, "Go home," commanded Bear.

Bear and Eric watched as the hounds ran back to the cabins."

"You trained them well," said Eric.

"Yeah, Thor and Odin will protect our families with their lives. Now, let's spread out and see what's got the hounds so worked up about."

Eric glanced back at the cabins, "Ma and Sara are standing at the cabin doors with rifles in their hands."

"Good," said Bear as he and Eric walked toward the ridgeline. As they got closer, Eric and Bear began moving from tree to tree.

Bear had just slid behind a small oak tree when a bullet slammed into the trunk inches from his head. The shot was followed by a volley of gunfire. When the shooting stopped, Bear yelled, "You okay?"

"A couple of close calls, but I'm alright."

Suddenly another round of gunfire erupted, "I figure six or more men," yelled Eric.

"Sounds about right," agreed Bear, "They got us pinned down. So, we must figure out how to attack them without getting killed."

Bear and Eric waited for another volley, but after several minutes, Bear said,

Eric, something ain't right. Why haven't they fired on us? Cover me. I'm going to try to get closer."

Eric waved to his father, then watched as Bear bent low

and dashed to a clump of bushes. Then Bear darted to a tree. Finally, when he was a hundred feet away, two men popped up and fired. Immediately, Eric returned fire as Bear hugged the ground.

"Pa, you okay,"

Bear gave Eric a quick wave and then crawled behind a rock. Taking a breath, Bear thought, *"I only counted two men. Where are the others?"*

Suddenly, gunfire erupted from the other side of the homestead, "Damn, they got around us and are attacking the cabins!

Seeing what was happening, Eric started running back to the cabins when a single shot hit him, and he went down.

"No!" yelled Bear, who fired back at the bushwhackers. Bear turned to run to Eric's aid, but then a wave of Eric's hand indicated he was okay.

"Thank the Lord, Eric is alive," exclaimed Bear.

Anger rose in Bear's throat, and he fired without taking aim, *"How the devil am I going to get out of this jam?"*

From across the fields, Bear saw Eric limp to Bear's cabin.

"Good, Eric's safe, but we're still pinned down," Bear thought.

An hour later, Bear was still forced to keep his head down. He had tried to charge the ridge many times but was driven back. Then Bear saw something that made his blood run cold!

Four men had rushed Sara and Eric's cabins. Using hatchets, they busted down the door and went inside. Sara had insisted that the cabin's entrance face the rising sun. Because of this, the doors to the cabins didn't face each other. So, neither Waity nor Eric could get a clear shot.

Bear cursed as the men ran out of the cabin carrying Lizzy, the couple's four-year-old.

Then ignoring the bullets that whizzed around him, Bear ran back to the cabins.

"Where are the hounds?" Bear wondered as he sprinted to the cabins. Bear entered his cabin to find Waity struggling to hold Eric down.

"Bear, help me! Eric wants to chase after the outlaws, but he's wounded and will bleed to death if he rides after the kidnappers.

"Eric," said Bear as he rested a hand on his son's shoulder, "Listen to me. You'll be no good to Sara or Lizzy if you're dead! Let your mother wrap the wounds. I promise I'll bring back Lizzy."

Weakened from blood loss, Eric collapsed in Waity's arms and cried. Waity, with tears in her eyes, said, "Go, Luv, and bring Lizzy home."

Bear ran to the other cabin. He found Sara and three-year-old Elmer sitting on the floor. Sara's hair was a mess, and she bled from her mouth and nose.

"Mommy's hurt," said Elmer.

"Yes, but she'll be alright," said Bear as calmly as he could.

"I tried to stop them, but they were too many," sobbed Sara.

"I know," replied Bear.

"Where's Eric? I saw him fall, but everything happened quickly, and he was gone the next time I looked."

"Eric was shot, but he'll be okay. Waity is tending to him."

"This is the worse day of my life! My husband was shot, and my daughter was taken!"

"I know, Sara, but I promise I'll find Lizzy and bring her home. Now, stay in the cabin. There may still be some outlaws around."

Bear stuck his head outside and listened. Except for some noisy crows, the valley was quiet.

"The bastards! This was all a ruse to draw Eric and me away so they could steal one of the children, but why? And what happened to Thor and Odin? They should have fought off the attackers or died trying."

"I heard one of the hounds' yelps just before the men entered the cabin," replied Sara.

"Okay, stay here. I'm going to take a look around. Then I'll be back and take you to our cabin."

Bear followed the tracks left by the outlaws back to the woods. As he entered the forest, he heard his hounds whining and the sound of leaves rustling.

· · ·

"WHAT THE HECK?" thought Bear as he walked toward the noise.

Finally, he found Thor and Odin. The hounds had been caught in a fishing net. The more they struggled, the more tangled the hounds became.

"Okay, fellows, be still, and I'll cut you loose."

Bear quickly sliced through the netting. Freed of the net, the hounds shook and scratched themselves. Then they ran off in the direction of the attackers' trail. Bear had to shout three times before the hounds returned. Bear petted each one, "I know, big guys, you think this was all your fault. But it wasn't. We'll hunt down these varmints, and when we do, I might let you gnaw on them for a while."

Bear returned to the cabins, "They're gone, But they left a trail even a blind mouse could follow. I'll take Thor and leave Odin here. I doubt if the outlaws will be back. But just in case. I'll ride to the Yaquis and ask Chief Leyva to send some warriors."

Bear started to leave but froze when he heard the sound of horses approaching.

"Stay inside, and don't open the door unless it's me."

Bear stepped outside and breathed a sigh of relief as the Yaquis, led by Juan Leyva, rode up to the homestead. But when Bear saw who was with the Yaquis, he almost jumped for joy.

"Kit Carson, how did you...?

"I was in El Paso last night. My horse threw a shoe, and

when I stopped at the blacksmith shop, Ralph told me about seeing McGrew and six men ride out of town. I could only think of one reason why McGrew would need six cowboys: you. So, I headed for the Yaquis and asked my good friend Chief Leyva if he could spare a few warriors. But it looks like we're too late."

"I'm afraid so. The outlaws took my granddaughter Lizzy. I think they're trying to drive us off our land."

"Then it's not too late to be useful."

"Nope, I was just going after the bastards. Juan, if you don't mind, could you have some of your men stay here and guard the place? Eric is shot up, but he'll be okay, and I hate to leave the place defenseless."

"No problem, Bear," I will select my best warriors."

"Thank you, Juan."

Bear gathered his gear, kissed Waity, and was ready to ride in ten minutes. The trail left by the outlaws was easy to follow until they reached the main route into El Paso. Then the increased traffic obscured the outlaws' trail.

It looks like they're headed for El Paso, but I doubt it said Bear. "I think our best bet is to scout both sides of the road, looking for tracks that break away from the trail."

"I agree," said Kit Carson.

"Okay then, let's do this."

It didn't take long before a sharp-eyed Yaquis spotted the tracks of at least a half dozen men riding north. "This is their trail," said Kit, "From the direction they're traveling, my guess is they're heading to Fort Tenoxtitlàn."

"I agree," said Juan, "The fort is all crumbled down, but six men could easily defend it."

"Okay, Fort Tentoxtitlàn it is."

They rode steadily for several hours until they saw the fort's remains.

Kit Carson pulled out his brass spyglass and peered through it. "She doesn't look like much," explained Kit Carson. But it wasn't so long ago that this little fort was all that stood between the hostile Indians and the settlers."

"See anybody," asked Bear.

"Yep, here, have a look."

Bear put the spyglass up to his eye, "There are the bastards. Looks like I winged one or two. Nothing serious. One is wearing a sling on his right arm, and the other has his head wrapped."

"So what's the plan?" asked Kit.

"If'n they didn't have my granddaughter, I say we surround the fort and attack. But with Lizzy being held hostage, we can't risk shooting her by mistake."

"I agree," said Kit.

"McGrew knows we're here," said Juan, "Hard to surprise."

"That's true," said Bear, "But we can't just sit here twiddling our thumbs."

"Bear, you said earlier that McGrew stole Lizzy to get at you."

"Yep, that's right."

"Then maybe he wants to bargain with you."

"It's worth a shot, "replied Bear, "At least it will buy us some time. Okay," said Bear, "I'll go in and see what McGrew wants."

"Get McGrew out in the open, and I'll blow his brains out," said Kit.

"Damn it, Kit. Let me see if I can talk to him. We have McGrew outnumbered and surrounded. He has no place to go. But the most important thing is the safety of my grand-daughter."

"Okay, of course, Bear," replied Kit, "It's your call."

Bear handed Kit his rifle. Then he lifted his hands and kicked the pony gently with his heels. Slowly Bear rode toward a gap in the fort's wall. Thor trotted next to Bear, growling.

"Easy now, Thor. You'll get your chance soon, but until then, no biting! Bear had trained the two Irish Wolfhounds to respond to hand signals.

"I hope you remember your lessons cause it's time for a test. Bear signaled Thor to crawl and watched as the Irish Wolfhound crouched low and began creeping toward the ruins."

Bear was halfway to the crumbled-down fort when a rifle barked, and a bullet slammed into the red clay dirt not ten feet away.

"That's close enough," yelled McGrew, "What do you want?"

"I want my granddaughter."

"You'll get your granddaughter back when you leave the valley," replied McGrew.

"McGrew, your days of running roughshod over EL Paso are over. We have you surrounded. You have two choices, release my granddaughter and surrender. I promise you and your men a fair trial. Or leave here, boots first."

"I'll give you credit. Willis. You've only been here a short time, and you've managed to stir up all kinds of trouble. I could use a man like you. Join me, and I'll make you rich."

"I rather dance with the devil! Now hand over my granddaughter!"

Out of the corner of his eyes, Bear saw Shotgun Rogers standing ten feet away. In one hand was his ten-gauge scattergun, and with the other, he grasped Lizzy's arm.

Bear's blood started to boil as he looked at his granddaughter. Lizzy's hair was a mess of tangles, and her face was dirty. Bear could see where Lizzy's tears had streaked down her face.

"Grandpa!" cried Lizzy as she tried to break free of Shotgun Rogers' grip.

"It's all right, Lizzy. I'm taking you home. Just as soon as I talk to Deputy McGrew."

"If you've harmed her." hissed Bear, "I swear I'll skin you alive and roast you."

"What do you take me for, Willis? I don't hurt children."

"Then prove it by releasing her."

"I told you my terms. Now it's all up to you. I'll let the girl go once you and your family are packed and ten miles out of El Paso."

"That's not going to happen!" snapped Bear.

"I'm not unreasonable, man, so I'll give you till noon tomorrow. If you still won't agree to my terms. I'll sell little Lizzy to a Mexican, who assures me the girl will fetch a good price."

Bear wanted to strangle McGrew, "Then you leave me with no choice! Thor attack!"

Instantly there was a blur of grey as the wolfhound leaped at Rogers. At the same time, rifle shots from Kit Carson and the Yaquis dropped three of McGrew's men. Fortunately for McGrew, he was unharmed as he was sheltered by Bear's body.

Bear focused on rescuing Lizzy. Thor had attached himself to Rogers' long black coat. Rogers let go of Lizzy and hit the hound on the head with his shotgun. The blow knocked Thor out. Lizzy ran to Bear, who hugged her, "It's alright, sweetie, I have you."

Lizzy buried her face into Bear's shoulder and wept. Bear heard a shot and watched as a bullet slammed into Roger's chest. Rogers went down, but to Bear's amazement, Roger's rolled over and scrambled away.

Bear wanted to go after McGrew and Rogers. However, his first concern was getting Lizzy to safety and seeing if Thor was still alive. Reaching Carson and the Yaquis, Bear sat down and cradled his granddaughter. "It's all over, Lizzy. Soon we'll be home."

"But Thor," sobbed Lizzy, "Is he hurt?"

Bear was about to reply when he heard a whimper, and Thor placed his head in Lizzy's lap. "Thor, I knew you'd be okay," said Lizzy.

She started petting Thor when she cried out and lifted her hand, which was covered with blood. "Grandpa, Thor's hurt."

Bear examined Thor's head, "It's just where that bad man hit Thor. He'll be okay, won't you, big guy?"

Thor responded by wagging his tail.

Kit and Juan approached Bear, "We shot four of McGrew's men and killed two. The other two cowboys escaped with McGrew and Rogers."

"I can't believe it," said Bear. "I saw Rogers get shot right in the chest. He went down, but he recovered and got away."

"Yeah," agreed Juan, "I'm the one that shot him. The rumor is Rogers has a steel plate under that frock coat."

"That would explain it," said Kit, "What do you want to do now?"

"First things first, I have to get Lizzy home. Then I'm going after McGrew and Rogers."

"Leave that to us," said Kit.

"No! I have a score to settle with those two polecats."

"Alright," agreed Kit, "But at least let us track them for you. If we don't, they could lose us up in the mountains."

"Okay, agreed Bear, "I shouldn't be more than a couple of hours."

Bear scooped Lizzy up and handed her to Juan. Then Bear mounted his horse. Juan lifted Lizzy and placed her behind him.

"Hold tight, darling, and we'll be home soon."

THE FIRST RAYS of the sun were peeking over the hills when Bear caught up with Kit and Juan. They had made camp by one of Franklin Mountain's many streams. Bear dismounted and squatted down next to Kit.

"I bet your daughter was happy to see Lizzy," said Kit."

"She and the rest of the family were overjoyed. I appreciate your help. I couldn't have done it without you and Juan."

"Glad to be of assistance," replied Kit.

"So where are they?"

"Two miles up the draw, McGrew Rogers and two of his men."

"Okay, then, I best get to it?" said Bear.

"How do you want to do this?" asked Kit.

"You two can take out the two cowboys, but Rogers and McGrew are mine."

"Remember, Rogers, is wearing that iron plate," Juan said.

"Then I'll have to aim lower," said Bear.

"I suggest we ride about halfway to their camp, then go

the rest of the way on foot," said Kit, "Only take your pistols and knives. Rifles make too much noise."

Bear, Juan, and Kit tied up their horses and walked the rest of the way to McGrew's camp. They were close to the camp when Juan held up his hand. They could see the campfire's flickering light through the brush and hear one of the outlaws laugh.

"Did you see that big mountain man's face when you crawled away? It was like he saw a ghost."

Rogers rapped on his chest, "Best investment I ever made."

Again, there was laughter, "Sounds like they're drunk," whispered Juan.

"All the better," hissed Bear, "I'll charge straight in, and you and Kit come in from the sides."

"Hopefully, they'll surrender," said Kit.

"Hmm, we'll see," replied Bear, "get in position, and on my signal, we go."

Bear watched Juan and Kit move to their spots. Then he raised his hand and dropped it. Like the grizzly he was named after, Bear charged through the brush. At the same time, Juan and Kit did the same.

"What the devil?" shouted McGrew going for his gun.

Bear fired, and the pistol flew from McGrew's hand.

The two cowboys seeing McGrew shot, raised their hands., "Don't shoot. We're just the hired hands!" one of them pleaded.

However, Shotgun Rogers decided to fight it out. He

drew his shotgun and pointed it at Bear. But Bear fired twice at Rogers, aiming below Rogers' waist. The bullets narrowly missed Roger's armor, hitting the outlaw in his groin.

With a scream, Rogers dropped his shotgun and grabbed his groin, "You bastard," Rogers cried.

"I ain't a smart man," admitted Bear, "But I ain't stupid."

"I'm bleeding to death; please help!"

"Yep, I 'spect you are," said Bear, tossing Rogers a handkerchief, "but there's not much I can do about it."

Bear, Juan, and Kit watched as Rogers took the handkerchief, pressed it to his groin, and tried to stop the bleeding. But it was a lost cause. Soon Rogers heaved a sigh and toppled over, dead.

Three days later, Kit Carson shook Bear's hand, "Well, Bear, I must say my life has certainly been more interesting since I met you."

Bear laughed, "I'm glad I could provide you some entertainment."

Everyone shared the laugh. Then Waity handed Kit a small basket filled with fried chicken and biscuits, "For the trip home," Waity said.

"Well, thank you, ma'am. And if you and your husband are ever in Taos, please feel free to stop by."

Kit mounted his horse, "I got a feeling we'll be seeing each other real soon," said Kit. Then he touched the brim of his hat and rode away.

"What did he mean, "We'll be seeing each other real soon?" asked Waity.

"I have no idea," replied Bear.

XXXXXXXXXXXXXXXXXXXXXXXXXXXXXXXXXXX

"I HOPE you enjoyed "Bear Willis & Kit Carson: Texas – Do or Die!"

Please consider leaving a review on Amazon @ Amazon.com: Peter Alan Turner: Books, Biography, Blog, Audiobooks, Kindle

THANKS,

Peter Alan Turner

OTHER BOOKS BY PETER ALAN TURNER

Bear Willis: Mountain Man Series

Chet Henderson: Texas Ranger Series

Willie McGee: Series

Zach Watkins: Mountain Man Series

Remington Ryder: US Marshall Series

I have also been honored to Co-Author several Westerns with some of the top Western Authors.

Bear Rasslin': A Bear Willis - Marshal Shorty Thompson Western Adventure (A Bear Willis: Mountain Man Novel Book 9) - Kindle edition by Turner, Peter Alan, Thompson, Paul L.. Literature & Fiction Kindle eBooks @ Amazon.com.

Jubal Stone: US Marshall – Blood in the Texas Badlands with Casey Nash

Jubal Stone: US Marshall – There Will Be Blood with Casey Nash

Bloody Rendezvous with T.E. *Barret*

Land Grab with Charles Ray

Hell or High Water with Jackie Paxton

Fearless: Twenty-Five True Stories of Fearless Frontier Woman w/Korra Turner

The Great Western: A Mountain Man Adventure Peter Alan
Turner w/Korra Turner

Contact Information:

Webpage: Westerns Books by Peter Alan Turner (western-books.com)

Amazon.com: Peter Alan Turner: Books, Biography, Blog,
Audiobooks, Kindle

Facebook: (2) Peter Alan Turner | Facebook

Email: pete@western-books.com

Listen to my podcast at Dusty Saddle Round-Up, where I discuss
Old West lore, history, and interesting little know facts. I also
interview Western Authors. Dusty Saddle Round-Up is available
on Audible, iHeart, Spotify & at Buzzsprout

Join "Pete's Posse" & receive a Free Western Short Story:

"Riding for the Pony Express"

Join Pete's Posse (mailchi.mp)

Made in United States
North Haven, CT
10 October 2023

42608477R00089